Not Forgotten
in Hollywood

Leonie Gant

This novel is a work of fiction. Names, characters,
businesses, places, events and incidents are either the
product of the author's imagination or used in a fictitious
manner. Any resemblance to actual persons, living or dead,
or actual events is purely coincidental.

ISBN-13: 978-0-9943999-1-5

Dedication

To Mike, Samuel and Nicholas. Thank you for your
unwavering support.

.

Chapter One

"You know, I'm really trying not to let it get to me, but you've never actually jumped on the bed over me," Griffin remarked dryly.

I hadn't realized that in my excitement I had started bouncing.

"I jump on the inside when it comes to you."

"Sure you do. So what is it about this job that has got you so excited?"

I looked at him incredulously.

"I am going to be working with Dorothy Stanhope. The Dorothy Stanhope. You know, Little Dottie. She was a child actress from the forties. I used to watch her movies all the time. I love her movies. Seriously, how could you have been brought up in LA and not know about Dorothy Stanhope?"

Griffin shrugged. "Unless she committed a crime she doesn't come under my jurisdiction."

"Well, I'm taking this job."

"Just keep in mind the reason you are usually hired," he warned.

I refused to concede that point.

"It's different this time. The reason she needs a personal assistant is because she is a recluse. The woman has had the same staff for decades. There is loyalty there. Believe me when I say that the people I normally work for don't even know the meaning of that word. She has known Monique for years so she trusts her to find the right person. This job isn't like my normal ones. This one is a reward for all the lousy jobs I've been given over the last couple of years.

Griffin looked doubtful.

I didn't blame him. I was usually assigned by Monique

to clients who had difficulty in keeping staff. Usually this was because I worked for celebrities who believed their staff should work for the privilege of breathing the same air as they did. I was generally called in by their management when the situation had become dire. I was ostensibly hired to be a personal assistant, but my primary job was to protect the brand from self-destructing in a spectacular, non-recoverable way. Monique Petit had realized a long time ago that providing staff that were used to the sometimes volatile nature of celebrities could be a lucrative business. A celebrity isn't an island. There were a huge number of people who were invested in these sometimes highly strung artists.

Over the last couple of years I had proved to Monique that I was willing and able to tackle her worst cases. Knowing how much of a fan I was of Dorothy Stanhope, she had given this assignment to me and nothing was going to stop me taking this job. I had been dealing with narcissistic crazies for too long for me to let this pass.

"I thought you were going to take some time off to start organizing the wedding," Griffin said calmly as he buttoned up his shirt.

I couldn't help the guilty feeling that went through me. We had been engaged for a month and I hadn't even started looking at the process of getting married. I had a feeling that my lack of enthusiasm was beginning to concern Griffin. According to his father, Lee, who had decided long ago that Griffin's and my relationship was community property, Griffin wanted to 'lock me down tight'. Of course, that statement could have more to do with Lee's desperate need to see his son married and happy. Lee Griffin wanted his son to have what he had been denied, thanks to Griffin's socialite mother who had decided that being married to a cop and mother to a baby wasn't how she had imagined her life. She had abandoned them soon after Griffin's birth thus creating a bit of an emotional desert for the two men in the Griffin family.

According to Lee, I was the ray of sunshine that both he and his son needed.

"I will," I said. "As soon as this job is over, I'll tell Monique I need a bit of time and I'll organize the wedding."

Griffin dropped a kiss on my head.

"Good."

I smiled as there was a knock on the door.

"Has Crystal learned how to knock rather than letting herself in with the emergency key?" asked Griffin wryly.

"She's happy to knock now," I waved my hand airily. "I think she just had the goal of seeing you walk out of the shower in a towel on her bucket list. Now that she's accomplished that, she doesn't need to do those surprise visits.

Griffin grimaced. Personally I didn't blame my slightly demented friend. Griffin walking out of a shower with just a towel around his lean hips always counted as a highlight of my day.

I opened the door and the smile on my face died.

"Hi, Trudie."

For the first time in my life I was truly struck dumb. Of all the situations I had expected to face, this was not one of them.

"Who is it, honey?" Griffin asked as he walked up behind me.

My brain knew I had to start talking but my mouth had decided to go on strike.

In front of me was my ex-fiancé, Paul, who deserted me while I was laying in a hospital bed and when I needed him most. Behind me was my current fiancé who thought that I was unnecessarily delaying the planning of our wedding. Well, this was awkward.

"This is Paul," I finally managed to croak out.

Griffin stuck out his hand and Paul grasped it. Griffin obviously did not realize exactly who Paul was. Not surprising since I hardly ever spoke about the man who

3

broke my heart and, until I met Griffin, destroyed my belief in happily ever after.

"You sound Australian. Are you a friend of Trudie's from back home?"

"I'm her fiancé," Paul announced.

That was one way to introduce yourself.

"Ex-fiancé," I said, trying to get control back over my vocal chords.

Griffin dropped Paul's hand, stepped in front of me and put his hands on his hips.

"I don't know what you're doing here but I would suggest you walk away."

"I need to speak to Trudie."

"I really don't think you do."

One of the things I loved about Griffin was that you always knew where you stood with him. Right now, Paul was standing on the edge of a precipice. It could go either way. I pushed myself in front of Griffin.

"What do you want, Paul?"

"Like I said, I need to speak to you."

"Why?" I asked incredulously. "I haven't seen you in a long time and the last time I saw you, you did all the talking. What could you possibly have to add to that now?"

The last time I saw my ex-fiancé I had been in a hospital bed with a bruised spinal column and no feeling in my legs after a run in with a drunk driver. Showing an exquisite sense of timing, Paul had decided at that moment that the devotion we'd supposedly had for each other since we were children was not enough to tie him down to a crippled wife. He'd crushed my sense of self and walked out of the hospital room, leaving me to pick up my life and start a new one.

"We never discussed things after you got out of hospital," Paul said while keeping an eye on Griffin who I just knew was glowering behind me. "You just disappeared one day, not a word to me. How do you think that made me feel? I admit I reacted badly, but after all we've been to each other, I deserved better than that."

I couldn't believe it. "What you deserved was a punch in the face. I didn't do it because I am a lady. I didn't let my dad do it because he would have killed you. I didn't let my Grandma do it because she wanted to use a set of brass knuckles."

"We need to talk," Paul repeated stubbornly. He had that look that I knew well. The one that told me that even if he left now, he would be back again until we talked through his issues.

"I can't talk now. I've got to go to work." How I wanted to go back to my excitement of ten minutes ago before Paul turned up and ruined it. "I'm not interested in talking to you. I want you to leave."

Paul glanced down at his bag which was next to him. Not for the first time I marveled at the thinking processes of some people. "I was hoping you'd provide somewhere to stay for an old friend."

"Hell no," Griffin said from behind me. I had to admit that I echoed the sentiment.

"You are not staying here," I said very clearly. "If you are staying in this city you will need to find somewhere else to sleep."

"I know that's not how your mother taught you," said Paul.

Paul was right. In the town I came from we all stuck together. If any other person from that town had turned up at my door I would have immediately organized a bed and meal for them. That included Old Bluey who was the town drunk. He stumbled daily from his home to the local pub, crossing the street at the same corner, at the same time every day. Everyone in town knew to slow down at Old Bluey's corner because, regardless of the road rules, he had right of way. He only bathed irregularly when the pub closed its doors to him because the smell was too pervasive. I would have opened my home to Old Bluey and fumigated when he left. That was what my mother taught me.

"Well," I was proud of the fact I spoke with a calm I was not necessarily feeling. "According to my parents, all those rules they taught me go out the window when you walk through the door. You, my friend, are the exception that makes that rule. In fact, my parents would be more upset with me if I let you stay here than they would be with the fact that I'm kicking you out."

"I know that your mother doesn't like your new boyfriend."

I felt Griffin tense behind me. I had to give Paul that one. Mom wasn't overly fond of Griffin.

"That may be," I said, "But Griffin's stuck by me through a lot and you never did, so in my eyes, what he wants matters so much more than what you want. And right now I'm pretty sure he wants you to get on the next plane back to Australia."

To be perfectly honest, I was pretty sure Griffin wanted to throw Paul in jail. Unfortunately, he didn't have that option. Yet.

"Go, Paul. Whatever you have to say, I'm not interested in hearing."

I was surprised to see a flash of hurt cross Paul's face. I was having trouble understanding why he would turn up here. Our lives had become completely separate a few years ago. To me, this blast from the past was coming completely out of the blue.

"I'll go," Paul said firmly. "But we need to talk about this, Trudie."

He picked up his bag and walked away. I closed the door and waited to see how Griffin was going to react to this unexpected turn of events.

"What was that all about?" Griffin sounded calm but I was very much aware that wasn't really how he was feeling.

"I have no idea," I said, feeling deflated.

"Why is he here?"

"I don't know. Maybe he heard that I was engaged

again."

"I thought your relationship with him was over."

"It is." I was trying to be reassuring because I could see that Griffin was beginning to lose it. "I haven't spoken to Paul for years. When my mom was here she said he'd been out to speak to my dad and had said that he may have made a mistake, but I never expected him to fly all the way here. Who does that?"

"A man determined to get you back does that."

I could see uncertainty in Griffin's eyes. "I don't want him. You know that, don't you? I want you. I'm marrying you."

"But now you have a choice," Griffin said softly. "He was the one you loved for most of your life. Can you honestly say that there isn't a part of you that wonders what it would have been like if he hadn't walked away?"

"But he did walk away. That told me everything that I needed to know about that man. If he wasn't strong enough to stick with me through something like that, then there was no way that I wanted to try to make a life with him."

Both of us fell silent. I knew there wasn't anything that I could say that would make this better.

"Kind of wish we could turn back the clock about twenty minutes," Griffin murmured quietly.

"You and me, both."

I wrapped my arms around Griffin's waist and laid my head against his chest. "I love you. Nothing changes that. I meant what I said. I don't care what Paul wants. You are what I want. I would never have said yes to marrying you unless I was totally sure."

"I know."

I looked up into those green eyes that always made me melt. Today, despite his words, I could see doubt in them. I hated that Paul had managed to do that.

Chapter Two

Staring up at the massive house in front of me, I knew that I had finally reached the place I had always wanted to be. Along with an utter fascination, some would say obsession, with old Hollywood, I adored the architecture of the older homes. I could have spent the next week just wandering around the grounds of this grand old property. You could see the effects of age that were weathering the mansion, but in my eyes it just served to make it more beautiful.

"You planning on going in, Missy, or do you just want me to work around you?"

I started at the irritated voice that came from behind me.

"I'm sorry," I said, although I really wasn't. I was a little annoyed that this man had interrupted my moment of delight at my situation. I was beginning to get back my joy which had been so unceremoniously destroyed by Paul. I had decided, when it came to my ex-fiancé, I was going with denial. I couldn't fix that situation so I was going to studiously ignore it.

I stuck out my hand. "My name is Trudie Eyre. I'm here to work for Miss Stanhope for a little while."

The man looked down at my hand and then back up at my face. He hesitated for a moment before grasping it. I didn't blame him. I was pretty sure I was wearing an almost hysterical smile. It can't have been comforting.

"I'm Eugene. I'm Miss Stanhope's driver and sometimes gardener."

I pumped his hand enthusiastically. "Hi, Eugene. I am so pleased to meet you."

Eugene retrieved his hand as soon as he could. Yep, I'd managed to scare him. I really needed to tone down the excitement.

He frowned for a moment. "I didn't realize that Miss Stanhope had decided to take on more staff."

I was quick to reassure him. "I'm only here temporarily."

I didn't want Eugene to think for one moment that I was a threat to his job. That was one downside to doing temporary work. You were sometimes viewed with suspicion by longstanding employees. Usually I didn't have to worry about that because most of my clients weren't able to hold onto staff long enough for them to fit the definition of longstanding. To be perfectly honest, the staff of most of my clients barely managed to be temporary. Staff would take a job because they thought it would be glamorous and exciting. Then they met the celebrity from hell and made their escape. Those placements were more likely to fit the definition of a drive-by.

Eugene kept his eyes on me. "You can just go up to the door and ring the bell. Just wait for a few minutes. It takes Martha a bit of time to get to the front of the house. Don't hit the bell again too quickly. She hates that."

"Thanks for the tip." I gave him another smile, hopefully a little less maniacal than the previous one, and strode up to the front door.

Taking Eugene's advice, I hit the bell once and waited. And waited. I started an internal debate as to whether I should ring the bell again when the door creaked open. If I hadn't been so excited, that creaking door to the old, slightly dilapidated house would have sounded ominous.

An elderly lady, her back ramrod straight, peered up at me. "Can I help you?"

I tried to put forward a calm smile. No point in me scaring all of the staff. "My name is Trudie Eyre. I was sent by Monique Petit to work as an assistant to Miss Dorothy Stanhope."

The woman looked me over. I hoped I passed muster

because I had a feeling if this woman wasn't happy with me, there was no way that I was going to step one foot in this house. I really wanted to get into this house. She opened the door, just wide enough for me to slide past her.

My breath caught as I gazed up at the sweeping staircase that faced me. During my years in Hollywood I had been in many beautiful mansions and I had been impressed many times. But those houses had been modern, decorated by the latest and most expensive interior decorators available. In the process those beautiful houses had lost something that this house had in abundance. They had lost their soul, if they ever had it. This house, despite the obvious work that it needed to have done, was filled with history. I could quite happily live in this house for the rest of my life. I was in love. Considering how Griffin was already feeling about my excitement about this job, I should probably avoid explaining my deep and instantaneous affection for this house. I had a feeling he wouldn't really understand.

"Follow me." The woman strode purposefully down the hallway and I fell in behind her.

As we made our way very slowly through the house, I decided that I should probably work at making a better impression than that of slightly crazy fan. I couldn't deny that I was a slightly crazy fan, but I had to at least try to maintain an air of professionalism.

"I'm sorry but I think I missed your name." I knew she hadn't given me her name but I was trying to be polite.

She didn't even look up at me. "I'm Martha. I've been Miss Stanhope's housekeeper for a long time. Everything here works well so don't even think of trying to change anything."

We both fell silent. Her, because she had obviously said everything that she needed to say. Me, because really, what can you say to that? Also, considering I had managed to build my excitement level up after my nasty surprise at home, nothing was going to be able to bring it down again. We finally made it to a room with a solid wooden door. Martha knocked on it with a lot more strength than I would have credited her with.

"Come in." I knew that voice. That voice had been in every movie that I loved as a child.

Martha grabbed the door and swung it open. I followed her through it while holding my breath and praying that I wouldn't embarrass myself too badly. There, sitting at the desk, was my childhood idol. For some reason I had been expecting to find her reclining in a full length gown on a chaise lounge. I blamed a completely overactive imagination for that expectation. What I got was an elderly woman hunched over in front of a computer screen, tapping madly away at a keyboard. When taking into account the fact that the rest of the house and furniture looked like it was still in the 1950s, the scene was a little incongruous, to say the least.

"Miss Stanhope…"

"What is it, Martha?" Then she stopped and stared at the screen. "No, that wasn't supposed to happen. I can't be dead."

Unable to quite process what was happening, I stayed silent.

Dorothy Stanhope, queen of the silver screen, my one and only celebrity hero, looked up at me with devastation in her eyes. "I was so close."

"It's a game," Martha drawled. "Just start again."

Dorothy Stanhope stood up and came out from behind the impressive screen. "You are failing to grasp how important this is."

"Not the first time," mumbled Martha. She cleared her throat. "This is Trudie Eyre, the assistant that the agency sent to you."

I held out my hand. "Miss Stanhope, I can't tell you how much of an honor this is."

The actress grasped my hand. I was surprised at the

11

strength in it considering Dorothy Stanhope was in her early eighties. Unlike the rest of Hollywood she hadn't aged as well as medical intervention would have ensured she did. Her gray hair looked to be in urgent need of some attention and she was dressed in stained clothes which, though comfortable, looked like she had been wearing them for days.

Dorothy Stanhope looked me over but her eyes kept wandering back to the screen. "That's wonderful. Could you please start Trudie off working in the attic," she said as she dropped my hand and headed back to the computer. She put a set of headphones on her head and started hammering away at the keyboard again.

Martha inclined her head to the door and I followed her out with a wistful look at Little Dottie. Martha closed the door behind us and we stood staring at each other. I drew in a long breath. Alright. That had been a little underwhelming. I was not, however, going to let it dampen my excitement.

"It's good to see her keeping up with technology." I couldn't think of anything better to say. I was still trying to process what had just happened.

Martha snorted indelicately. "She plays online computer games. Plays them constantly throughout the day and night. I don't understand it."

Of all the situations I had expected to encounter, this was new. I jumped when I heard yelling coming from the office.

Martha turned around and started walking away. "Don't worry about it. Some kid probably got in her way. She doesn't cope well with that."

Okay. I was going to need to work on some of my more unrealistic expectations about this assignment.

I frowned. "What exactly am I supposed to be doing?" Monique had been a little vague about the details of this job. In my excitement over working with Little Dottie Stanhope, I had ignored that oversight. I was beginning to think that I should have asked some more questions.

Martha sighed, some impatience spilling through. "As you can see, this house is not in the best of condition. For years the only people who have worked here have been Eugene and myself. We sometimes get in other staff, but generally it has just been us. It has got to the point where it is too much for us. Miss Stanhope does not want any more staff so she is considering selling the house. The house isn't in the best of condition so we've had contractors in to look at some renovations to bring it up to date. While they were evaluating the house they found a section of the attic which had been separated from the rest of the house. As far as we know, nobody has been up there in decades. At this stage it looks like there are mementoes from her early career. We need you to go through the attic and catalog everything. Miss Stanhope wants to start selling off some of her memorabilia to help finance the renovation of the house.

I almost stopped breathing. If you looked at it negatively, I was going to be spending the next several weeks working in a hot dusty attic, cleaning out old junk. I, however, preferred to look at the situation as I was going to be examining the memorabilia from Little Dottie's movie career. The excitement level which had taken a hit when I walked into the office was now back up again. I followed Martha into the library. It was everything you thought a library should be. Dusty shelves lined all of the walls, full of hardcover books.

"Any chance these need to be cataloged too?" I asked, trying my best to appear nonchalant.

Martha peered at me. "You're a keen one, aren't you?"

I tried to give a calm, gentle, professional smile. Martha walked to one of the walls and fiddled with the side of one of the bookshelves. There was a creaking sound and the bookshelf swung out revealing a stair case behind it. I felt my mouth go dry. There was a hidden door to the attic. This could not be any more perfect.

"I hope you're not easily spooked," Martha said drily.

I shook my head confidently. "Not at all."

Martha reached to the side and pulled out a torch and some bug repellant. "Here are your tools. According to the contractors there is a light up there that actually works, but some of the corners are still dark."

That explained the torch. "And the bug spray?" I queried as she passed it over.

"The contractor that went up there cleaned most of the cobwebs away, but there are still some creepy crawlies up there. Hope you're not afraid of spiders."

"Not at all," I repeated. To be perfectly honest, I was deathly afraid of spiders. I come from Australia where a good proportion of the spider population could do very bad things to you. I had always reasoned that a fear of spiders was the smartest thing I could have. But there was no way that I was going to let that fear stop me from going up into the secret attic. I gripped the torch and the bug spray tightly, and started to make my way up the stairs.

Chapter Three

At the top of the stairs I looked around at what was a surprisingly large room. It was hard to believe that this much of the attic had been sealed off and nobody had noticed. All around me were trunks and boxes, piled high in a haphazard fashion. It was going to take ages to catalog everything that was here. I flipped open the lid of the nearest trunk and started coughing as the dust that had previously settled on the lid swirled around me. Underneath sheets of newspaper which were dated in the late forties I found dresses, one of which I recognized from a Dorothy Stanhope movie from when she was a child actress. I remembered dancing along to the songs of that movie when I had been a child.

I grabbed my phone and started dialing my best friend, Crystal. This kind of moment had to be shared.

"You are not going to believe where I am," I said excitely, not even giving her a chance to say something.

"Trudie?"

"I am in Dorothy Stanhope's secret attic and I am surrounded by costumes and props and things from every single one of her early movies that I have seen."

"Why are you whispering?" asked Crystal.

"I don't know, it just seems appropriate. I have never been so excited in my entire life."

"I'm sure Griffin would be pleased to hear you say that."

"You know what I mean. I can't believe Monique gave me this job. This is every dream I had coming to Hollywood come true. I would do this job for free if I had to. I think I'm going to swoon."

"Did you just use the word 'swoon'?" asked Crystal.

"Yes I did, because that is the only word that is

appropriate for the setting that I am in right now."

"You know, sometimes I forget that you're a country girl from Australia, and other times it is so obvious," Crystal sighed. "Speaking of Australia, I met your friend from back home."

That gave me a bad feeling.

"What do you mean, you met my friend?"

"Your friend who came to visit you. I told Miss Betsy a friend of yours had turned up and she let him rent out that spare apartment she keeps for a week. We had a chat for a while before I went to work. Seems like a really nice guy. I invited him for dinner if you wanted to come over. It will give me a chance to find out all the juicy embarrassing stories from when you were a kid."

I felt my heart sink again. This was going to teach me to be a little more open about my past with my friends. I had told Crystal and her husband, Edwin, about my former fiancé once during an ice cream binge session which had got out of hand. I don't remember if I had actually used his name. I may have called him the dumbass, or a variation thereof. Lesson learned.

"Did he by any chance mention who he was?"

"Sure," Crystal said. "He's your friend from back home, Paul. Didn't you get to see him before you left for work? Was it supposed to be a surprise?"

I grimaced. "Oh, it was a surprise all right. I think he missed out on one vital piece of information. The guy you're so keen to invite to dinner is my ex-fiancé, Paul."

There was silence. "Why is this the first I am hearing of this?"

I shrugged and then remembered that she couldn't see me. "I had to get to work and I didn't expect it to be an issue."

"Not an issue. Are you kidding me?" I had to pull the phone away from my ear as Crystal's voice rose in pitch. "The man who deserted you in your hour of need, who ripped your heart out of your chest and flung it away. Are you telling me that I invited him to dinner?"

I really didn't want to answer that question because Crystal seemed to be getting a little worked up all on her own about Paul. I didn't think that I needed to add to it. There was silence as I tried to work out the best way to calm this conversation down. After a few tense moments I realized there wasn't a way to make this situation better.

"Yes, my ex-fiancé, Paul, turned up this morning and said he wanted to speak to me. I said no, Griffin said 'hell no' and we sent him on his way. I was kind of hoping never to see him again so I'm probably going to turn down your dinner invitation."

I could hear Crystal choking on her end of the phone. "You think I'm going to allow that person into my house now that I know who he is. I'm going to contact Miss Betsy immediately and get him kicked out."

My stomach clenched as I felt a bit bad that Paul was going to lose his accommodation. LA was definitely not the place to be if you had nowhere to sleep. Despite what I'd said earlier this morning, I did feel a little guilty that I hadn't let him stay. "Don't do that. I don't think he'll be staying for long. If he stays out of my way and, more importantly, away from Griffin, it won't matter if he's staying there.

Crystal cleared her throat. "Remember the discussions we've been having about the fact you are too nice and need to put forward what you want rather than making other people happy."

"Yes," I muttered, so pleased that we had now moved to discussing my character flaws.

"This is one of those moments. He did you wrong so he doesn't get to stay in our building."

That sounded like the beginning of a country song. Strange that it was coming from a Hollywood princess.

"I think you should stay out of this," I warned. Crystal had been brought up the pampered daughter of one of the top casting agent's in Hollywood. Despite that, her rebellious teenage years had nurtured a mean streak in her which could translate into some difficulties for Paul while he was here.

"Don't you worry about it," said Crystal in a tone of voice which was guaranteed to cause me to do nothing but worry about what her next step was going to be. "I'll have a chat with Miss Betsy and we'll work out what the best course of action should be."

Now I was really worried. Miss Betsy was the owner of the apartment complex that I lived in and a former stuntwoman with quite a few skills which regularly caused me some concern. The idea that those skills would be pointed in Paul's direction made me very nervous.

"Please, Crystal. Before you do anything I want you to ask yourself whether it is something that I would do."

I could almost see the eye roll through the phone. "That limits me in a way I'm not comfortable with." It always worried me when Crystal started speaking in a semi-formal manner.

"Just don't do anything until I get home and we can talk this through." There was silence. "Please, Crystal."

Crystal huffed. "Fine. We don't do anything until we speak to you but there is nothing stopping us from making plans that we can implement quickly if need be, is there?"

I knew a compromise when I heard it and I also knew it was the best deal I was going to make today.

"I can live with that."

Crystal grunted in a very unladylike manner. I had a feeling that the self-control I was asking for was going to cost her.

"Thanks Crystal," I said quietly.

"For what?"

"For being so mad at him on my behalf." Sometimes it felt good to know that there were people who were always in your corner, no matter what. It made me feel like I could handle anything, even Paul.

Crystal's voice softened. "I'll see you tonight, when you

get home from work."

I laughed as I looked around the attic. "If I get home from work. I may just hide out here for the next few weeks. I have no problem doing that at all."

After Crystal got off the phone I tackled the job at hand. With my laptop in one hand and the trusty bug spray in another, I worked my way slowly through the first box. I did have some knowledge of the memorabilia market and while working, my mind was doing rough calculations of what these items were worth. I could see Dorothy Stanhope getting quite a lot of money for these memories. I couldn't believe they had been put away so long ago and then forgotten. But then, considering the full life she had led, maybe these items didn't hold the same importance to her that I was attaching to them.

"Trudie." I heard Martha call up the stairs.

"Yes," I replied as I wiped the sweat that had started dripping in my eyes.

"Would you like some lunch?"

I looked down at my watch. I couldn't believe that the morning had flown by so quickly. A part of me was frustrated at the slow progress that I seemed to be making. Another part of me was enjoying myself too much to care.

"I'll be right down," I called back. I stood up and dusted myself off as well as I could.

At the bottom of the stairs Martha looked me up and down and frowned slightly. "Maybe you should have lunch on the patio."

I followed her gaze and was not surprised to find streaks of dirt on my clothes. "It's a little dusty up there."

"Hmm."

As I looked out over the gardens I could see what Martha had meant by the property becoming too much for her and Eugene to handle. A good proportion of the garden was becoming overgrown and I could see from Eugene's movements that he was being hampered by painful joints.

"How long have you both worked here?" I asked.

Eugene looked up from the sandwich he had been eating. "I started working in the gardens while I was still in school. I guess that makes it about sixty years or so.

Wow. For someone who jumped from assignment to assignment, I had to respect someone who could stick with the same job for that long.

"How about you, Martha?"

Martha sighed as she put her sandwich on the plate. "I haven't worked here as long as Eugene but I was brought up in this house, along with Miss Stanhope. My mother worked for Miss Stanhope's mother as the previous housekeeper."

"So you knew Dorothy Stanhope when she was doing the Little Dottie movies?" I really wished I could tone down the excitement a little.

"Yes," Martha said shortly. I waited for more but she returned to eating her sandwich.

"Did you ever get a chance to go on set with her?"

"Yes."

This was killing me. I wished Martha would be a bit more forthcoming with her information.

"I've found a lot of things from the forties and fifties in the attic," I said. "At the moment it is mostly costumes, but I've found a few props from the movies she did as well. Some newspaper clippings, photos and letters. It's amazing what is up there. I can't believe that all those things went missing for so long and nobody noticed."

Martha shrugged, obviously less impressed than I was with what had been found.

"I'm a big fan," I confided quietly.

Eugene raised an eyebrow.

"I would never have guessed," Martha said with what I thought was a touch too much sarcasm.

The rest of the lunch passed in silence. I tried to start conversations a couple of times, but neither Martha nor Eugene seemed to be interested. After finishing off my sandwich I stood up, eager to remove myself from what was becoming an awkward situation.

"Thanks for lunch."

Martha nodded her head in acknowledgment.

After a moment of uncomfortable silence I smiled. "I'd better get back to work."

Both Eugene and Martha stared up at me.

I smiled again, turned around and headed back for the house.

Chapter Four

Once I was up in the attic with the dust and the spiders, I felt more comfortable. It was obvious that I was considered the outsider here. I guess after decades of knowing each other and working together, I was seen as an annoyance that they had to put up with until the job was done. I pulled another box down and opened it. I found piles of paperwork and started flicking through them. I was having trouble seeing the writing in the low light of the attic so I pulled out my trusty torch. As I pointed it at the box my eye was caught by a wicker chest in the corner. It was large and unusual and, to my mind, looked like it would definitely hold something more interesting than paperwork. I hurriedly put the papers back in the box, closed it up, and pushed it to one side.

I walked over to the chest and ran my hand along some of the wicker on the front panel. I knelt down and pushed open the lid. The age of the chest made it difficult and the hinges groaned in protest as they opened for what I was sure was the first time in years. The top layer, like the other boxes I had opened, consisted of old, yellowed newspapers from the fifties. I carefully peeled away the layers of paper, eager to find what treasures this chest held. When the last layer came away my breath caught and I wished I hadn't eaten that sandwich. I pulled away and took in some deep breaths. Once I no longer felt the real need to empty my stomach on the attic floor, I looked back into the chest. There, crammed in tight, was what could only be described as a mummified body. A part of me hoped that it was some kind of sick prop used in a movie, but the stains on more newspapers that were crammed around the body made me doubt that wild hope. From the scraps of clothes on the body I could tell that it was male. Other than that it reminded me of documentaries that I had seen about ancient cultures and their embalming techniques. I fumbled in my purse and pulled out my phone. With shaking hands I dialed the number of the one person I needed in a moment like this.

"Hey, beautiful."

I breathed a sigh of relief. Just hearing my fiancé's voice was always enough to calm me down.

"Griffin, I've found a body."

I could almost see Griffin go on alert. "Where are you?"

"I'm at work."

"Have you called 911 yet?"

"I think it might be a bit late for that."

"You never know, Trudie. Sometimes they look dead but the paramedics can get them back."

I looked down at the mummified remains in the chest.

"I am definitely sure that the paramedics aren't going to be able to do a thing with this one."

"Are you in a safe place? Can anyone get to you?"

I could hear Griffin moving as he fired questions at me.

"I'm in a secret attic in Dorothy Stanhope's house. I just found a body that looks like it has been here for a very long time."

"Does anyone else know what you've found?"

"No."

"Keep it that way. I want you to stay where you are. I'm coming for you."

"Okay," I said quietly.

"I need to make some calls, sweetheart," Griffin said. "If anything happens I want you to call me back straight away. Can you do that?"

"Yes."

"I'll be right there."

He hung up. Once again I was alone with the chest and its gruesome contents. As much as I tried to avoid it, I couldn't stop my eyes from returning to the body.

Questions raced through my mind. Who could this person be and why on Earth was he stuffed in a chest in Dorothy Stanhope's attic? I looked down at my hands. They were still shaking. Considering my past history with finding dead bodies, you would have thought that I would be coping with this better.

While waiting for Griffin I looked down at my phone and made a decision. Chances were it wasn't necessarily the right one, but it made me feel like I was doing something in what was now beginning to feel more and more like a tomb.

"Ma petite, it is so good to hear from you. I hope you're enjoying your assignment. What can I do for you?"

Monique sounded happy. I really hated to be the one to bring down that happiness.

"Uh, Monique."

"No," Monique said sharply.

"No, what."

"I know that tone in your voice. I specifically chose this assignment for you as the safest one possible."

"I'm safe," I said. "That's not the problem."

Monique sighed in relief. "Thank goodness, I thought for a moment there that you were going to report that you had come across some unfortunate soul."

I was silent while I tried to work out how I was going to explain this.

"Trudie?" I had obviously let the silence go on for too long.

"I've found what looks like a mummified body in a chest in Dorothy Stanhope's attic." I generally found rushing my words helped in situations like this.

"You found what?"

Sometimes it didn't.

"I was cataloging boxes that have been in a secret attic in Dorothy Stanhope's house for years and I found a body stuffed in one of the chests. I have called Griffin and he is on his way now. I am perfectly safe. Nobody in this house knows what I've found."

"Your next assignment is working in my office."

"Actually, I was hoping I could get some holiday time to organize the wedding." I know, totally the most inappropriate time to discuss organizing time off work, but if it distracted Monique from her plan to permanently hobble my career, I was going to go with it.

Monique was silent for a moment. "Are you okay, ma petite?"

"Not really," I said, surprised to feel tears prickling the backs of my eyes. At this point I was going to blame the dust. "It's just taken me by surprise."

I heard loud voices coming from the house below. "I think Griffin is here. I'll get back to you later."

Hanging up the phone, I raced down the stairs at the same time that Griffin walked into the library. I had to hide my distaste when I saw that he was followed by his new partner, Detective Desmond Pickett. I wasn't overly fond of Detective Pickett. I personally blamed him for the regular nightmares I had been having for the last month after he used me as bait for a killer. Despite what my friends thought about me being too nice, Detective Pickett proved that I was perfectly capable of holding a grudge.

"What have you done?" Martha's accusing tone came from behind the two large police officers.

"I found something in the attic that I felt required legal attention," I said shortly. After finding a body I wasn't quite feeling like indulging the fangirl side of myself.

"You okay?" Griffin asked.

I nodded. "It's up here."

I turned around and the two police followed me up the stairs. I still had the torch on me and pointed the light towards the trunk.

"There he is."

The two men looked down and Pickett whistled. "Now that is interesting."

Not exactly the term I would use. I personally thought

horrifying was more appropriate.

Pickett looked over at Griffin. "I'll call it in."

Griffin nodded and Pickett headed down the stairs. The second we didn't have an audience Griffin opened his arms and I stepped into them.

He wiped a finger across my dirt streaked cheek. "Looks like you've had a bit of a rough day."

"Not quite the dream job I was expecting," I said ruefully.

"It seems I'm going to get to meet the great Dorothy Stanhope after all." He looked down at me. "How did it go for you?"

I shrugged. "A little underwhelming. Seems she's a hard-core online computer gamer these days. Doesn't seem to pay attention to anything else." I shook my head. "I should have known better. How many times have I told you that meeting a celebrity is, for the most part, disappointing?"

Griffin pulled away. "So what were you doing that led to finding a body stuffed in a chest?"

I took a shallow breath. "From what I've heard, this attic was only found recently while getting quotes for renovations. There are a lot of boxes that need cataloging so that is my job. Going through all of these boxes and sorting them out, hopefully so that Dorothy Stanhope can sell what's in them and fund the renovations."

Griffin grimaced. "So how long has this attic been unopened for?"

"From what I understand, we're talking decades. I've only been through a couple of boxes but the thing is that they're all lined with newspaper. I haven't seen any of those newspapers being later than the 1950s."

"That's a lot of years ago." Griffin looked pensive as he glanced back down at the body. "I have to admit that I've never seen a body like that before. There's a possibility it has been here the entire time."

I felt sick. Imagine living in a house with a dead body in

the attic for at least sixty years. I pulled away from Griffin when I heard Pickett's heavy tread coming up the stairs.

"We got someone from the Coroner's office on the way," he announced. "Seems when you use the word mummy with those guys they get a little excited."

Griffin glanced up at Pickett. "If you want to stay with the body and wait for them, I might go downstairs and have a chat with the staff."

Pickett nodded.

"I'll come with you," I said hurriedly. I was not really keen on staying in the attic with a dead body and a man that I was not particularly interested in making small talk with.

Chapter Five

I was not surprised to find both Martha and Eugene waiting in the library, speaking to each other in low voices. I hung back as Griffin stepped forward and pulled out his badge.

"I'm Detective Griffin from Homicide. We seem to have found a body in the attic. Would either of you have any clue as to why it is up there?"

If first impressions counted for anything, I would have bet money that nothing Griffin said could have shocked those two more.

"A body," exclaimed Martha. "Who is it?"

"I was hoping you'd be able to tell me that," replied Griffin.

Martha shook her head. "We didn't even realize that part of the attic had been walled off until recently." She glanced at Eugene. "Neither of us is in any condition to climb those stairs. The contractor and Trudie are the only ones who have been up there."

Griffin raised an eyebrow at me. I shrugged. Wouldn't be the first time I had been questioned in relation to a dead body. Although the speed with which Martha had chosen to point to me as a potential suspect was truly impressive.

Griffin cleared his throat. "I am going to need to speak to all of you separately, including your boss."

Martha and Eugene exchanged a look. I had a feeling they were wondering how they were going to be able to get Dorothy Stanhope out from behind her computer.

Griffin looked around the library. "In a very short period of time this area is going to become quite busy. Is there somewhere I can go to conduct interviews?"

Martha hesitated.

I could see Griffin's features tighten. "Or we could do this down at the station."

And there was the threat. I hoped that Martha wasn't feeling obstinate today. It would be nice for me not to end up in an interrogation room.

Martha indicated the room opposite the library. "I'm sure you'll be more comfortable in the living room across the hall."

Griffin inclined his head and strode out of the library. I could see Martha and Eugene glancing at each other nervously. It wasn't every day that people got interviewed by the police because of a dead body. I could understand their trepidation.

"I'll go first," I volunteered. After all, I did have all the experience.

Griffin looked up in surprise as I walked into the living room. I sat down on the couch opposite him.

"You can go, Trudie. Can you please send the gardener in?"

I was slightly taken aback by the dismissal. "What do you mean, I can go? That's not how we do things. Where's the unpleasantness? Where's the arguing? Where's my interrogation?"

"Did you kill the mummy in the attic that looks like it's been there since before your parents were born?"

"Of course not."

"I believe you, interrogation done."

That was slightly anticlimactic. I walked into the hallway and nodded at Eugene. "He'd like to speak to you."

Eugene's face took on a sickly green color as he closed the door behind him.

"That was quick." Martha eyed me suspiciously.

"I'd given all my information when he first arrived."

"Hmm."

I didn't think she believed me but I wasn't going to enlighten her about my relationship with Griffin.

"Has anyone told Miss Stanhope what has happened yet?"

Martha shook her head. "I've called her lawyer. He's really the only one she listens to these days." She looked towards where a noise was coming from the front of the house. "Speak of the devil," she muttered.

I followed her gaze. Two men strode towards us, cloaked in the mantle that proclaimed a lifetime in the legal fraternity.

"What have you done this time, Martha?" sneered one of them impatiently.

I stiffened and moved forward wanting to put myself between Martha and the truly unpleasant individual who had just arrived. I needn't have bothered. Instead of stepping back and hunching in on herself like a lot of people do when confronted with that sort of aggression, Martha was standing tall, her eyes spitting fire. Although I barely knew her, I knew there was some serious history happening here.

"I'm the one who called the police."

The man turned slowly in my direction. He looked to be the same age as Martha but age had not diminished his presence. "And who exactly are you?"

"I'm Trudie Eyre. I've been hired by Miss Stanhope to catalog the items in the attic upstairs. I found a body and called the police immediately. Martha only just found out what I had done."

The sneer that had been directed at Martha was now firmly pointed in my direction.

"You called the police," the lawyer said slowly. "Let me get this straight. You only started working here today and you took it upon yourself to call the police. You didn't think to inform your employer or any of the staff."

"Yes, sir." I met his eyes coolly. This man was a bully. That much was glaringly obvious. Even if I hadn't seen Martha's reaction to him, the contempt in his voice when talking to me would have clued me in to his nature.

Luckily, or unluckily for me, I was used to dealing with bullies.

"Everything okay here, Trudie?"

I was surprised at the concerned note in Pickett's voice. Of all the people I expected to come to my rescue, I would have to say that Detective Pickett was low on the list.

"Detective Pickett, what a surprise to see you here." It looked like the two men were acquainted with one another.

"Mr Harrington, what can we do for you today?"

"I'm here to ensure my client is protected from the farce that represents law enforcement in this city."

To Pickett's credit he smiled widely. "Of course, Mr Harrington. Detective Griffin is currently conducting preliminary interviews. Once we've spoken to staff we will be wanting to speak to Miss Stanhope. It will be your choice whether that interview is done here or down at the station."

I watched as Harrington's face turned a dull shade of red. He spun around and stalked off. The other man followed with Martha running along behind him.

"I glanced over at Pickett. "Nicely done."

"Martin Harrington is the worst kind of lawyer there is. He's a thug and he represents everything bad that you think about lawyers. I'd hoped he'd retired by now." Pickett frowned. "I'm kind of surprised to see him here."

"Maybe he's a friend of Dorothy Stanhope. That might be enough to bring him out of retirement. Who was the guy with him?"

"That was his brother, Avery Harrington. I don't know much about him. He's a bit younger than his brother and he's a bit less flamboyant in the way he does his work."

The door to the living room opened and Eugene stepped out. He paused when he saw Pickett and me standing there. "Where's Martha?"

"The lawyer arrived and she went with him to speak to Miss Stanhope," I replied.

Eugene's face tightened. It seemed Martin Harrington was quite popular everywhere we turned. Without a word he headed towards the front of the house.

"You really do have the most interesting workplaces," commented Pickett.

"I only started today and within a few hours I found a body and called the police in to interrupt their peaceful lives. I won't be surprised if I'm fired within the next few minutes." This wasn't exactly how I had been picturing this day going. Not for the first time today I wished I could go back to the excitement I had felt earlier this morning.

Griffin poked his head out and looked wary when he saw that Pickett and I were standing together. He was very well aware that I was not fond of his new partner.

"Where's the housekeeper?"

"The lawyer turned up so Martha went with him to see Miss Stanhope," I offered helpfully.

"It's Harrington," Pickett added.

Griffin grimaced. "I thought he was retired."

I wondered if that was a genuine belief or a vain hope. Considering the way Pickett and Griffin were reacting to Martin Harrington, I had a feeling that Harrington turning up was going to be counted as the worst part of their day. And that included the part where they saw the mummified body.

"I believe you want to speak to me, Detective."

I hadn't realized that Martha had walked up while we were talking.

Griffin smiled tightly. "Yes, could you please come in? This shouldn't take long."

He walked back into the living room and Martha followed him. At the doorway she turned and faced me, her expression grimly set.

"Trudie, Miss Stanhope asked me to let you know that your services will no longer be required for today. She will be contacting Miss Petit regarding your continued employment."

That did not sound good.

"Are you sure there isn't anything else I can do?"

"I believe you've done quite enough already." Martha closed the door firmly behind her.

And that set me in my place. I wish it didn't surprise me that I could last months in jobs where I was absolutely miserable and didn't want to be there, but the second I found a job that I really wanted, it looked like I'd managed to get myself fired on the first day.

Pickett cleared his throat. "Anything I can do to help you?"

I was really not in the mood to deal with the new and improved sensitivity of Detective Pickett.

"Just tell Griffin that I've finished up for the day," I muttered. All I wanted to do was go home and drown my sorrows in a tub of ice cream. For a day that had started out with such promise, I had hoped for a better ending.

Chapter Six

If I had hoped that my day would improve with the promise of ice cream, I was sadly mistaken. I found Miss Betsy waiting in the parking lot, concern etched on her face.

I had barely managed to get out of my car when Miss Betsy started.

"I am so sorry, Trudie. I didn't even think that he was the same young man. It didn't even cross my mind. If I had realized, there is no way that I would have rented a place out to him."

I knew that. I knew my friends and there is no way that any of them would do anything to cause me any discomfort or pain. The fact of the matter was that Paul was part of my past. I had told my friends about him but he wasn't a subject I dwelt upon. I'd told them the reason behind a small part of my craziness, but then it wasn't a topic that I felt like re-visiting. I wasn't surprised that they hadn't realized who he was and I was sure that he had purposefully neglected to fill them in. That didn't bother me. What was done was done. What did bother me was the shimmer of tears that I could see in Miss Betsy's eyes. Before she became my landlady, Miss Betsy had been a stuntwoman in Hollywood in a time when they were considered a little more expendable than they were now, legally speaking. It made her one of the toughest people I knew. This woman who had managed to freak me out by showing me how easy it was to break into my apartment, and carried a gun like it was a natural extension to her hand, had tears in her eyes. In that moment I saw red. I was angrier with Paul than I had been in a very long time. How dare he cause Miss Betsy to cry.

"Don't worry about it. I'll sort it out," I murmured as I

gave Miss Betsy a quick hug.

After finding out which apartment Miss Betsy had given him, I marched over to face my ex-fiancé. I pounded on Paul's door, a little heavier than I may have intended. Seems that during my time with Griffin I had learned the police knock.

He opened it and smiled widely when he saw it was me.

"Hey, Tru, I'm glad you came. Do you want to come inside?"

That was the very last thing I wanted. I knew at that moment that there was at least one set of eyes focused on this door. There was no way I was going to follow my ex-fiancé into an empty apartment. I would never hear the end of it.

"I'm staying out here, Paul. Look, I need you to leave. The landlady isn't happy about you being here. To be perfectly honest, no one is happy about you being here, including me."

Paul leaned against the door frame, his arms crossed, smiling at me. I'd forgotten how cocky he was. "You know something, if my being here didn't bother you, you wouldn't be here right now. I think that you're remembering how good we were together."

I crossed my own arms. "I don't deny we were good together. You were my best friend from the time I was four years old. I worshiped the ground you walked on for most of my life."

Paul smiled widely.

"But that ended when you weren't there for me." I watched him incredulously. "You don't get it, do you? Walking out on me wasn't one of those things we can gloss over. I don't want a man who is only there for the good times. Life is uncertain. I want the man I end up with to be strong enough to weather the bad times as well as the good.

Paul ducked his head. "I know I messed up, Tru. I was young and overwhelmed."

"I was young too, but I dealt with it because I had to." My hands curled into fists as I tried to remember why I was putting myself through this. "You said you wanted closure. I don't understand why you came all the way here to get it, but you were always stubborn. If you want to know if I forgive you, then I do. I want you to have a happy life. I don't want you to give me or what happened between us another thought."

I waited expectantly. I figured that speech had covered every contingency.

Paul looked me over and his eyes softened. "I still love you, Tru."

My breath caught. I simply had no way to deal with that information. "You can't," I said, turned around and walked away.

I knew that I was heading to my apartment but I wasn't really looking where I was going. That explained why I ran right into Sean. He grabbed my arms and steadied me. I looked up into his concerned eyes. In the year since I had met him, Sean had grown from a small gawky red-headed teenager to a tall, lanky, gawky teenager. When I met Sean he had been living on the streets after being thrown out of home by his mother. He was currently living in a small apartment in the block, going to school, and sometimes helping Miss Betsy with maintenance in return for rent and food.

"Are you okay?" The sympathy in his eyes was almost overwhelming.

I gave him a tremulous smile. "I'm fine. Just been a bit of an interesting day."

"The ex?" Sean nodded knowingly, although considering he was only seventeen years old I wondered exactly what experience he was bringing to the table.

"It's nothing."

"Do you want to talk about it?" he asked.

No, I did not want to talk about my romantic disaster with a teenage boy.

Sean put a sympathetic arm around my shoulder. "You could take me out for a coffee and we could get something to eat."

I should have seen the ulterior motive. Sean had reached that level of development when the only two things on his mind were girls and food. Every now and again food edged out girls for the number one spot. Looked like today was one of those days.

"Fine, I'll feed you."

Sitting at the diner, I had to admit that I was impressed with the amount of food such a lean kid was able to put away. While I sat nursing a coffee, Sean made his way through a fair portion of the menu. After what seemed like ages he leaned back with a satisfied smile on his face.

"So, you going to tell me what's going on?"

"No."

"Come on. I already know some of it. What you need is someone who can give you some input without getting emotional."

"What do you mean?"

"Miss Betsy and Crystal are acting like this is the worst thing that can possibly happen to you."

"What do you think?" I couldn't help myself. I was a little curious to see his opinion.

Sean looked at me, his expression serious for a change. "You've been shot. If you could get through that, I think you could handle just about anything."

I took everything I'd been thinking back. Sean was right. I was letting myself get too caught up in the drama of my ex-fiancé coming back in my life. I had faced far worse things than him walking out on me and I was still able to hold my head high and tackle every day. And it took a teenage boy to cut through all the garbage.

"You are absolutely right," I said quietly.

Sean grinned, the cockiness of youth shining through. "Knew I was." He popped some more food into his mouth. "So, when do you think that Griffin is going to arrest him?"

"Griffin isn't going to arrest him."

Sean snorted. "The second Griffin finds out that your ex is living in the same building, he is going to go nuts."

"I thought you said that this wasn't a drama."

Sean nodded wisely. "For you it isn't. But you have a tendency to think these things through eventually. Griffin is a whole other matter."

I put my coffee down and looked at Sean with a new-found respect. He may be young but he was smarter than I had been giving him credit for.

"I'll just explain to him what the situation is and that it isn't something to worry about. It isn't like Paul is going to end up living here. He has got to go home eventually."

Chapter Seven

As I opened the door to my apartment, I hoped that what I had told Sean was true. I did not want my past to cause problems for Griffin. I kept telling myself that it didn't cause problems for me but I still kept seeing Paul's face when he told me that he loved me. After Paul had walked out on me there had been far too many days when I had imagined that exact moment. The moment when Paul realized what a mistake he had made. A part of me that I was not too proud of had fantasized about him crawling back to me, begging for forgiveness. I had believed that those thoughts, ones that I looked back on now with a certain sense of shame, had left me a long time ago. I tried to tell myself that what he said didn't matter, but to a certain part of me it did.

My phone rang and I looked down to see it was Monique. I guess this was the moment that I was going to get fired. I couldn't control the disappointment I was feeling. I had really wanted this job.

"Hi, Monique."

"Why did you not tell me your ex-fiancé turned up?"

Not how I was expecting this conversation to start.

"Aah…"

"My Reggie is currently looking at his visa status to see what we can do to get rid of him. We can't allow him to disrupt your life with your man."

"What?" I was having trouble catching up to this conversation. I wasn't surprised that Monique had learned of Paul's arrival back in my life. There was very little in this town that got past her. To be perfectly honest, I would not have been surprised if she had found out about Paul's arrival before I did. I was, however, a little shocked at the way she was going in to bat for my current relationship.

Monique had never been one of Griffin's greatest fans. In fact, you could probably say that she was the opposite of one of his greatest fans. Her husband, Reggie, wasn't that fond of Griffin either.

"There is no need to overreact. I am sure that he will be leaving soon." I hoped with everything in me that he would be leaving soon.

Monique sighed patiently. "Ma petite, a man does not fly half way around the world simply to say hello."

Unfortunately, Paul had done a little more than just say hello.

"I can handle it."

Monique sighed again. I had been noticing her doing that a lot with me lately. "You aren't getting it, are you, ma petite? You don't have to handle this on your own. You have people who love you and want to take care of you."

I could feel my eyes prickling with heat. That was so sweet.

"I need to talk to you about the Dorothy Stanhope job."

I couldn't believe that such a sweet moment was going to be followed up by me being fired.

"She doesn't want me back, does she?"

"You haven't lost the job as such," Monique said carefully. "Although her lawyer was keen to see you kicked out."

I wasn't surprised by that. I had a feeling that Martin Harrington was not someone who gave second chances.

"So they want me back?"

"We're just going to continue on a day by day basis. As soon as the police are finished with the property you will be returning, but your duties may be slightly different. You may also be subject to a little bit more oversight."

I grimaced at the thought of Martin Harrington hanging over my shoulder. This job was definitely not reaching any of my expectations.

"If you have any problems, I want you to call me

immediately."

"Thanks, Monique," I said gratefully. "And please don't let Reggie do anything without passing it by me first."

Monique gave a very uncharacteristic grunt which did not fill me with confidence and hung up.

Looking down at my phone I couldn't help but smile.

"You look happier than I was expecting."

I hadn't even heard Griffin walk in.

"I'm just remembering not to sweat the small stuff."

Griffin put his arms around me and placed a soft kiss on my lips. I closed my eyes and enjoyed the moment.

"You finished work for today?"

Griffin nodded.

"Want a coffee?"

"That would be great."

I busied myself making coffees while Griffin sat down, leaning his elbows heavily against the kitchen bench.

"Are you going to work tomorrow?" he asked.

"That depends on how long your people are going to be turning over that attic. You have told them to be careful, haven't you? Some of that stuff would be priceless to collectors."

"We're already out. You can go back there at any time."

I stopped what I was doing. "What are you talking about? You guys are never that fast."

"The Coroner has looked at the body and is pretty certain it is sixty years old. After that amount of time, there isn't much we can do about it."

"So, you're telling me that you're not looking into this case?" I was sure that I was misunderstanding something here. "This man was murdered, wasn't he? There is no way he ended up in that box under natural circumstances. Why aren't you hunting for his killer?"

Griffin wiped a hand over his face. "Sweetheart, you need to understand. We are struggling to keep up with the murders that are happening now. I get new cases being dropped on my desk every day. A murder that happened sixty years ago, where the killer is most likely dead themselves, is not a priority. We don't have the budget or the manpower to follow up on it."

I passed the coffee over to him. "A man was killed and nobody cares. That's wrong."

Griffin reached for my hand and squeezed it gently. "I am so sorry, sweetheart, but that's the situation we have. The case will be kept open and I'll be passing it onto the cold case squad, but without a deathbed confession from someone, I don't see this case ever being solved."

A part of me felt sick at the overwhelming injustice of it all.

"I wish I could give you better news. I know this isn't the kind of thing you like to hear."

It wasn't, but considering the way my day had been going, bad news about the murder seemed to fit right in. That brought me to a topic of conversation which, if I'd been able to avoid it, I would.

"There's something I need to tell you and I need you to remain calm."

Griffin put down his coffee and straightened in his seat. I could tell by the creases in his forehead that I may not have chosen the best way to start this conversation.

I nervously cleared my throat. "Paul is staying in LA for a little while.

"Where is he staying?"

I knew Griffin was not going to take this well.

"Crystal accidentally organized for him to get one of the apartments here for about a week. Miss Betsy wants to toss him out but he's refusing to accept her refund and it could get a little messy."

Griffin stood up resolutely. "You're damn right it could get a little messy."

I jumped up and stopped him as he strode towards the door. "No."

Griffin looked down at me and quirked an eyebrow.

"What do you mean, 'no'?"

"I mean you are not going to do anything about this. If you make a big fuss he's going to think that there are problems between us and you're not feeling secure in our relationship. If we just go on with our normal lives and ignore him, he'll go away."

"You really believe that?"

I shrugged. Believed, no. Hoped, definitely.

"I think I should speak to him."

That was the one thing I was really hoping to avoid happening.

"I already did that. I don't think it's going to make any difference."

I could feel Griffin tense under my hand. "You already spoke to him."

Uh oh. I really didn't like that tone.

"Exactly when did you speak to him?"

"When I got home, Miss Betsy was upset that she had rented him the apartment so I went over to see him to discuss the matter like adults. I just wanted to try to get him to leave before he caused any more disruption to the people that I care about." I glanced up at Griffin's stony countenance. I was obviously not getting through to him. He wasn't seeing the important part of my argument. "He made Miss Betsy cry. Nobody makes Miss Betsy cry. What else was I supposed to do?"

I could see Griffin taking in a deep breath. "What did you say?"

"I wished him a happy life. I told him I forgave him and that he could go on with his life without worrying about what happened between us."

"That all sounds great, but if he got his closure, why is he still here?"

I shrugged. To be perfectly honest, I wasn't really sure what Paul was hoping to accomplish by staying.

"What exactly did he say, Trudie?"

I had really hoped that Griffin wasn't going to ask me

that question.

"He told me he still loved me," I spoke softly, fully aware that sentiment was the very last one that Griffin wanted to hear.

Griffin stepped back. "He still loves you," he repeated.

"It doesn't matter." I wanted him to understand. "Paul has always acted impulsively. Something has probably happened recently and he has some regrets. We've known each other since we were kids. When anything went wrong I was always the default person he would go to because I would sort it out. It's just misplaced nostalgia. I'm sure that's all it is."

"You may be sure, but I'm not."

Griffin grabbed his jacket and started heading for the door.

"What are you doing?" I demanded, a little afraid that I'd lost control of the situation.

"I'm going to speak to him."

Why was it that of all the ways to deal with this situation, the man I loved had to choose the stupidest? Once again I was going to have to be the voice of reason. "I don't think that is the best idea."

Griffin turned around and put his hands on my shoulders. "Don't worry. I'm a cop, I talk to people for a living. I know what I'm doing."

As one of those people that Griffin had talked to, I had to say that my level of concern did not abate one bit at that statement.

"Please don't do anything that requires me to bail you out of jail, because I won't."

Griffin quirked an eyebrow at me. He knew that was an empty threat. He would have to make me really angry before I left him languishing in a jail cell. Surprisingly enough we hadn't quite got there in our relationship yet.

I followed him as he strode out of the apartment. I spotted Crystal and Edwin across the hall and raced over to them.

"I need you to go with Griffin," I said urgently to Edwin.

"Sure," replied my best friend's husband. "Why?"

"He's going to talk to Paul."

"No."

"What do you mean 'no'?" Up until this moment I would have thought there was nothing that I would ask Edwin that he would turn down.

"Have you really seen the size of the man you are going to marry? He is so much bigger than I am and he is a cop. There is no way that I am going to get between him and the man that you originally planned to spend the rest of your life with."

"I'm disappointed in you."

Edwin shrugged. "I can live with that disappointment."

I decided to try another tack. "I don't need you to get between them. I just need a voice of reason there." I paused for dramatic effect. "Please Edwin. You're the one person I can depend on to do this."

"Fine," Edwin sighed. "But you're covering any and all medical bills, up to and including therapy."

Crystal watched as her husband stalked away. "I won't be happy if any part of him is broken."

That was putting it mildly. If a hair on Edwin's head was harmed, then I would be answerable to Crystal. I really didn't want to be answerable to Crystal. I was pretty sure that would be unpleasant.

Crystal followed me back into my apartment and I sat down on the couch with my head in my hands.

"I can't believe what a lousy day I'm having."

"At least you haven't stumbled over a body."

I knew Crystal was trying to be supportive, but that was pretty much the worst possible thing that she could have said. I avoided her eyes as I remembered my day in the attic.

"You found a body?" There was that screeching quality in Crystal's voice that I seemed to be inspiring lately.

"I found a mummified body in Dorothy Stanhope's attic. According to Griffin it had been in there for about sixty years."

Crystal shuddered. "That's creepy."

Yes, it was. However, as an indication of how my day was going, it didn't come close to being one of the top things that was occupying my mind at the moment.

"Who was it?"

Considering how she usually reacted when I found a body, I was impressed with how calmly she was dealing with the situation.

"Nobody knows."

Crystal eyed me curiously. "For somebody who found a body today, you're showing a distinct lack of interest in what is happening with the case."

I shrugged. "According to Griffin, there is no case. The body is sixty years old. Any murderer is probably long gone and the chance of solving it is nonexistent."

"They're not even going to try to solve it?"

I shook my head, still disappointed by what I had been told. "I understand what Griffin is saying. When you compare a sixty year old murder with one that happened this morning, priorities have a tendency to shift. I just think it's really sad."

I glanced nervously at my door. If I didn't think that it would make the situation immeasurably worse, I would have marched down to Paul's apartment to tell both men to pull their heads in. The only thing stopping me was my Grandma Rita's advice running through my head. She had always said that getting between two men when their egos were involved was its own special brand of stupid.

"He'll be okay," Crystal said softly.

"I can't believe this is happening. I never thought for a moment that Paul would turn up again."

"Maybe he just wants to start a new life, and he's feeling that the bad karma from the way he treated you is dragging him down. Just forgive him and he'll get going."

"I already tried that. It didn't exactly work out the way that I wanted it to."

Crystal eyed me curiously. "What happened?"

"He said he still loved me."

I could see Crystal's jaw drop. "That jerk."

I raised an eyebrow.

"He's trying to manipulate you. You do see that, don't you? He knows that you're close to marrying another man and he's come here to sabotage it. Please tell me you're not going to fall for it."

"Of course I'm not going to fall for it. It just took me by surprise. It's been a long time since I heard those words from Paul. There was a time when I would have given anything to hear him say that. It took a long time for me to reconcile myself with the fact that I never would."

I could feel Crystal watching me curiously. "So how do you feel about it?"

There was the question for the day, if you ignored the other question about the mummy that I had found.

"I don't know yet," I said quietly.

"Wow," Crystal breathed.

I looked up as I heard a noise at the door. Edwin walked through with a somber look on his face.

"What happened?"

"You do know how to pick them, don't you?"

That sounded ominous. "What happened?"

"I know Griffin is a cop and has to deal with garbage all the time, but I never really understood the level of self-control that he had."

"What happened?" I had reached the point of panic and was ready to cause Edwin some real physical harm myself if he didn't start answering my question.

"Your ex just gave Griffin a thorough explanation as to why you two should be back together again. He informed him that he was just the rebound guy because you and he had been together almost your entire life. He finished it off by informing your current fiancé that now that he was back you would drop Griffin in a heartbeat."

"He said what?" I had always known that Paul had the ability to make dumb moves, I just didn't realize how dumb those moves could be.

"For a country boy, he was certainly waxing lyrical about your great love affair and devotion to each other. I've got to say that if any of Crystal's exes had spoken to me like that, I wouldn't have shown nearly the same amount of self-control that Griffin did."

Before Edwin I don't think Crystal had been in any relationships which had lasted longer than a couple of dates. I somehow doubted that Edwin had anything to worry about.

I headed towards the door. "Where is he? I need to talk to him."

Edwin grabbed my arm as I walked past him. "Don't, Trudie. I think he just needs a bit of time to let off some steam. He asked me to tell you that he was going to the gym. I'm guessing he needs to work off a little bit of that anger before he does something that he is going to regret. Or he might do something he doesn't regret and that could be worse."

I raked my hand through my hair. I couldn't believe this was happening. I knew Griffin and this was not something he was going to cope with well.

I felt Crystal's arms go around me. "Are you going to be okay?"

I nodded even though I didn't really feel like I would be. "I think I just need some alone time to work out how I'm going to deal with this mess."

She nodded. "We're at home if you need us."

I watched the two of them walk away. After going into my apartment I leaned my back against the closed door and slid down until I was sitting on the floor. I heard a message come through on my phone and glanced down at it. I wasn't surprised that it was from Griffin telling me that he would be going over to his father's house. If anything that gave me some indication of how upset he was. I never thought I would see the day that Griffin went to Lee for advice. In general, the two men avoided emotionally charged subjects with a passion they usually reserved for sports. I was a bit concerned about how well that conversation was going to go.

Chapter Eight

The next morning I blinked blearily as I looked over at the empty side of my bed. Considering the crazy hours that cops kept, this was definitely not the first time that I had woken up alone since Griffin and I had started going out. For some reason it seemed to be more significant this time.

After my shower I heard a knock at the door. I really hoped that Paul had not decided to try to resume our conversation. There were so many reasons for me to be mad at him that I wasn't really sure where to start. All I knew was that he was the reason I didn't get to sleep with Griffin's arms around me the previous night.

I opened the door.

"Heard your ex-fiancé is sniffing around."

"Hi, Lee."

"So what are you going to do about it?"

I turned around and headed for the kitchen. I definitely needed a coffee before being interrogated by my ex-cop, future father-in-law.

"There's nothing I can do about it. I don't understand why he's here and to be perfectly honest, I don't think I care that he is here."

"Your current fiancé cares." Lee accepted the coffee I automatically handed him.

I stopped making my coffee. "Griffin told you?"

Lee nodded and I eyed him suspiciously. "Did he send you here to keep an eye on me?"

Lee rolled his eyes. "Of course he didn't. I decided to do that all on my own. Not too impressed that he's turned up. Figured I'd get his measure."

I dropped my head in frustration. "You don't need to get his measure. You don't need to get involved at all.

Everyone's reacting as if this is some terrible calamity in my life. It isn't. Paul and I were finished years ago. There is nothing left there. You don't need to circle the wagons and you definitely don't need to protect me. I can handle this just fine."

Lee watched me thoughtfully. "You may be handling this but my son isn't."

"I know," I sighed.

"He doesn't react well to threats."

I cocked my head. "Really."

Lee chuckled. "No, he doesn't. At the moment he thinks your ex-fiancé is the biggest threat to him and you there is. Maybe give him a little bit of slack for the fact that he's acting like an idiot."

"Don't I always?"

Lee smiled but I could see his heart wasn't in it. "He loves you very much. You know that, don't you?"

"I know."

"Considering the amount of trouble you get into, I never thought one of your exes would be the problem."

I stayed silent.

"You found another body."

And there it was. "Yes, I found another body. Does that entitle me to another lecture today?"

Lee shook his head. "Mummified remains from last century don't count."

I smiled wryly. "I'm beginning to see that."

Lee shrugged. "It's the way the world works. The problems from now are going to be the ones that get the attention. Considering how stretched the department is, it would be irresponsible to try to solve a case as old as this."

I'd already been told that. I glanced at my watch. "I need to get going to work, Lee," I said gently.

Lee put down his cup and kissed me on top of my head. "I'll see you later. Please try to stay out of trouble."

I gave a non-committal smile which I hoped he would accept. The frown he gave me didn't indicate that he did.

As I looked up at the front of Dorothy Stanhope's mansion I marveled at the difference that a day could make. Yesterday I had been filled with excitement at this moment. Today, it was more trepidation. Despite what Monique had said, I had a feeling that my time working here was going to be short. I straightened my shoulders and rang the bell. I looked around as I waited and spied Eugene working in the garden. I raised my hand to wave and got a sharp nod in return. At least some things hadn't changed.

The door finally scraped open and I turned to find Martha's disappointed face looking up at me. "It's you again."

I hadn't been expecting a parade, but I really didn't know why this woman disliked me so much.

I pasted a smile on my face that I knew probably looked fake, but I didn't have the energy or the will to try to make it look real. "Good morning, Martha." I stepped past her as I walked into the house, only to be brought up short by the presence of a familiar figure.

"Good morning, Trudie."

If I had been asked to name the people that might possibly be standing in Dorothy Stanhope's house when I got there that morning, I could guarantee that Travis Cooper would not have even made it to the middle of that list.

"What are you doing here?" I croaked.

Travis smiled widely. "I've been hired to work with you."

I stood there with what I was sure was a stunned look on my face. I was having a little trouble processing what was happening here. I couldn't quite understand why the man whose greatest claim to fame was investigating cheating spouses would be helping me go through an attic of dusty relics.

"I'll leave the two of you to sort this out," murmured Martha. I barely noticed her leaving.

"You know, I wish you'd take that look of horror off your face," Travis drawled. "It's not doing much for my ego."

"What are you doing here?"

Travis looked around. "We need to talk and I would rather not do it here."

I followed him into the library and waited for an explanation.

"I've been hired to look into the body you found in the attic."

"By who?" I couldn't help the incredulous tone in my voice.

"Monique got in contact with me. It seems Dorothy Stanhope is hoping to find out who it is quickly and put it all behind her."

"Okay," I said slowly. "What does that have to do with me?"

"It has been suggested that your expertise is required."

"I'm working with you?"

Travis grimaced. "Not exactly. Monique believes I need an assistant for this case and since you are already here…"

"I'm working for you?" No, this was not happening. I realized that my dream job wasn't going quite the way I wanted it, but my eternal optimism had kept me believing that it was going to get better. Working for Travis Cooper was not getting better.

"I quit."

Travis looked at me sourly. "You do not quit. You never quit. I thought that was your reputation."

That was my reputation. I was well known for my ability to handle the worst of situations, but I'd had it. I was dealing with the disappointment of this job being nothing like I had imagined, Paul's unwelcome interruption in my life and being concerned with the way Griffin was handling it. Considering Griffin's feelings on the whole Travis Cooper situation, I could not see my working for him improving my life at all. There is a moment when everybody needs to know when it is time to toss in the towel. I had reached that moment. The best thing that I could do now was to admit I'd reached my limit, find a tub of ice cream, and hibernate for a few days or weeks.

"You're not going to quit," Travis repeated.

"I want to quit," I said heavily as I sat down.

Travis sat next to me and put an arm around my shoulders. "This isn't like you. Tell Uncle Travis what the problem is."

I grimaced. There was no way I was going to confide in Travis about my relationship problems.

"Is it because your ex-fiancé is in town? I'm guessing Griffin isn't handling it well."

I looked up in shock. "How on Earth do you know about Paul?"

Travis looked at me in disgust. "You seem to keep forgetting that I'm an investigator."

"You follow people and take pictures of them while they're cheating on their partners. We're not talking hardened criminals here."

Travis sighed. "You forget that isn't all that I do. It's just the part that brings in the most money."

I snorted indelicately. "Fine, I work for you. What exactly is it that you want me to do?"

"I want you to take me through what happened yesterday."

I stood up and headed for the bookcase. I had mastered opening the locking mechanism to the hidden staircase the previous day. As it swung open I heard Travis give a low whistle.

"Cool," he breathed.

"I know."

I felt the stirrings of excitement again as I walked up the staircase with Travis trailing behind me. He followed me into the darkened corner of the attic where the chest that had been holding the body still stood. I looked around and noted that nothing seemed to have been disturbed. That more than anything told me how little time the police had spent investigating this crime. From my previous experiences with homicide investigations, one thing I could guarantee was that after a police search there was always a mess left behind.

"Wow, they really didn't do anything, did they?" Travis said as he looked around the attic.

I shook my head.

"Okay, so we start from scratch." Travis pulled a file from his backpack.

"What have you got there?" I asked curiously.

"The file from the cops."

I was pretty sure he wasn't supposed to have that.

"How exactly did you get a crime file from the police? I really don't think you got it from Griffin."

Travis laughed. "No, Griffin isn't the kind of cop to hand that sort of information over easily, especially to me. I got one of my sources from inside the department to get a copy of this for me."

"How?"

"I went out with her once."

"And that was enough for her to risk her job to help you out?"

Travis spread his arms wide and gestured to himself.

"Wouldn't you?"

"I can guarantee it wouldn't be enough."

"Your loss."

I wasn't really sure that it was, but I figured I didn't need to destroy his ego on my first day working for him. I grimaced at the thought. Griffin was not going to like this at all.

"So what does your magical file say?"

Travis flicked through it. "Not a huge amount. They did find a wallet with a driver's license which, until we find out better, we can probably assume it's him."

I waited for a few moments. I could see how this man

could annoy people very easily. I was beginning to feel sympathy for Griffin that he'd had to work with him for an extended period of time.

"Are you waiting for a drum roll? Who is he?"

I could tell that charming grin on Travis's face was going to annoy me before the day was out. "His name was Giovanni Moretti. According to his license he was twenty-two years old. He had a total of ten dollars on him when he died, which contrasted nicely with the very expensive watch on his wrist."

"So, we're guessing robbery isn't the motive," I ventured.

"Unless he had something else on him that was worth killing for."

"Do we know how he died?" I asked.

"Not yet," said Travis. "The autopsy is being done today so we are going to need to go and get the results."

His confidence was beginning to wear on my nerves.

"And how are you planning on getting those results? It isn't like you can just walk in and demand them."

"It's okay. I dated one of the medical examiners once."

"And you think that means that she will just give you the information."

"Why shouldn't she?"

Travis looked perplexed at my lack of faith in him. Not for the first time, I wished I had an ounce of his confidence.

Chapter Nine

I shouldn't have been surprised when we were standing in the medical examiner's office and I found that Travis's confidence was in no way misplaced. The red carpet had been rolled out for him from the moment he arrived. Dr Mina Wills had almost stumbled over her own feet when Travis walked in. We had been in the office for a full ten minutes before she even realized that I was in the room. The look she gave me was a combination of loathing at someone she thought could be a rival, combined with envy that I was spending the day with the great Travis Cooper. I simply wanted to get out of there as soon as I could. While I could see why Travis with his gorgeous looks and easy charm could inspire that sort of devotion, I was fortunate in that it seemed I was immune to it. I was not, however, immune to the braying laugh that echoed through the room anytime that Travis said anything.

"So what can you tell me about our unfortunate victim?" he asked.

Dr Wills seemed to gather her professional persona around her. "The remains were in remarkable shape. It isn't often that we see a body like that. The victim was a male in his early twenties. He seemed to be pretty healthy. From what I could tell he was killed by a blow on the back of the head from something heavy. I don't think he stood a chance. I checked the dental records you organized for me." She smiled flirtatiously at Travis. "It is Giovanni Moretti."

Obviously Travis had already started his investigation. The man definitely worked quickly.

"Do you know when he was killed?" I interrupted.

"I would say we're talking decades," the doctor said with a slight amount of irritation in her voice. Once again I had the feeling she would have been much happier if I hadn't been here. "I do have a theory about that though."

Travis and I leaned forward at the excitement in her voice.

"The mummification of the body indicates that it was subjected to extreme conditions immediately after death. Combine that with the newspapers that surrounded his body, I think he was killed some time in the first week of September in 1955."

That statement seemed terribly accurate to me.

Travis cleared his throat. "Why would you think that?"

"In September 1955 Los Angeles was in the grip of a terrible heatwave. This body was found in an attic, in a chest. You put a body with newspaper packed in tightly around it, in an attic with little or no airflow, in the middle of a deadly heat wave, and that body would be virtually cooked." She looked at the two of us triumphantly. "That's one way you would make yourself a mummy."

Despite questioning her taste considering her obvious adoration of Travis, I was impressed with the way her brain worked. As well as slightly nauseated at her description.

Travis whistled beneath his breath. "That's amazing. I can't believe you put that all together."

Dr Wills positively beamed under his praise as Travis stood up.

He bestowed his winning smile on the doctor.

"Thanks, Mina. That has really helped."

And just like that the professional persona melted away again. "Anything you need, Travis. Just call me anytime."

As we walked out of the medical examiner's office I looked back to find Dr Wills watching us leave with an adoring look on her face.

"Seriously, did you rescue her puppy or give her a kidney or something?" I asked. "That level of devotion is disturbing."

Travis grinned widely. "It's a gift."

"No," I objected. "Musical talent is a gift. The ability to paint great art is a gift. Whatever you have going on is just plain unsettling."

I could tell from the look on Travis's face that I was not putting anything close to a dent in his confidence. I should probably learn to recognize a losing battle.

"So, what do we do next?"

"We speak to everyone in that house. From what I understand, Dorothy Stanhope is one of those few celebrities who has managed to keep staff for an extended period of time. They all date back to the period we are looking at."

"You think it was one of them?" I didn't think I was hiding the skepticism in my voice very well.

"You need to look at them as they would have been sixty years ago when the crime happened, not as the people they are today."

I wasn't so sure that was going to be much of a stretch. I was pretty sure Martha was capable of killing me if she put her mind to it. To be perfectly honest, it might be interesting to put up Travis's legendary charm against her taciturn personality.

Chapter Ten

Sitting across from Martha and Eugene, there was a part of me which appreciated that we had found a woman who was completely immune to Travis Cooper. It would have almost felt like we were part of a special sisterhood, except for the fact that it was blatantly obvious that she wasn't too fond of me either.

"Is this going to take long? We have work to do."

It was interesting to hear the slight emphasis on 'we' that Martha gave while looking in my direction.

Travis tried his most ingratiating smile. From the look she gave him it had as much effect as if he'd spat in her food.

"I know this has been a trying couple of days for you."

Martha glared at me. "We were fine until she walked through the front door."

Travis nodded sympathetically. "You would be amazed at how many times I've heard that."

I wish I could say I was surprised to see how willing Travis was to throw me under the bus. But I had to admit that it worked. Martha didn't give him the smile he was probably expecting, but the expression of pure disdain that she had been sporting eased slightly.

Deciding to take that as an encouraging sign Travis plunged ahead.

"As you are aware, Miss Eyre found a body in the attic in the course of her duties."

And there was another set of poisonous glances in my direction. This job was really not turning out the way I had hoped it would.

Travis hurriedly continued. "We are reasonably certain that the gentleman in question died in the first week of

September in 1955. Were you living here at that point?"

Martha paused for a moment as if thinking back, and then shook her head. "No, I had just started working as a secretary. My mother was still living here while she worked as a housekeeper, but because I had finished school and wasn't working here, I had to move out. I was living at a boarding house."

"That seems a little harsh," Travis commented.

"It was the way it was. It wasn't like my mother or I were family."

Even I could hear the bitterness in Martha's voice. It made me wonder why she was working here at all. You would have thought that sixty years would be enough time to push your way through that kind of anger. It seemed Martha was the kind to hold a grudge.

"How about you?" Travis asked Eugene.

"I've lived here my entire life."

Travis glanced at me. He had obviously heard the same wistfulness in Eugene's voice as I had.

"We have identified the body as being a Giovanni Moretti. Do you remember anyone with that name from that time period?"

If I hadn't been watching her so closely I wouldn't have seen the slight flinch Martha gave at the mention of the body's name.

She gave a tight smile and shook her head. "No, I don't remember anyone with that name, but it was so long ago."

That settled it. If Martha was throwing a smile in my general direction it could only mean that she was lying through her teeth.

Eugene looked troubled. "Can't recall that name."

"You're sure?" asked Travis.

Both Eugene and Martha nodded.

Travis pulled a couple of cards out of his pocket and passed it to the two staff members who were obviously lying to him. "Well, thank you very much. If you think of anything else that may be relevant, please do not hesitate to give me a call."

Martha nodded sharply and, with Eugene trailing behind her, she quickly left the room.

"I'll bet you money those cards will end up in the trash," I mused.

"Probably," mumbled Travis.

His lack of interest in the way Eugene and Martha had answered the questions he had asked confused me.

"They were lying, you did know that, didn't you?"

"Of course they were lying," Travis said with a slight amount of irritation creeping into his voice. Looked like he was enjoying working with me as well.

"Then why didn't you push them on it, you know, wear them down?"

"Unfortunately, I'm not a cop," Travis said tiredly. "I can't threaten two elderly citizens with arrest, keep them in a small interrogation room for hours on end, or do any of those other unpleasant things that cops can do to get a confession out of someone. I have to make do with my stellar investigative skills. That is how I will get this job done."

It was good to see that a fruitless interview was in no way able to dent Travis's confidence.

While Travis busied himself writing down far more notes than I thought that interview warranted, I had a quick glance at my phone and tried to squash the small feeling of disappointment. I didn't like that I hadn't heard from Griffin since he spoke to Paul. I was justifiably concerned at what could possibly be going through that man's head today.

I looked up when I heard a throat being cleared and was surprised to see Eugene in the doorway, that same passive look on his face.

"Are you busy?"

I tried to smile encouragingly at him. His expression didn't change.

Travis waved a hand at the seat opposite us and

Eugene sat down again. He looked uncomfortable to be there.

"Did you have something that you wanted to add?" Travis asked.

Eugene nodded.

"Did you know Giovanni Moretti?"

Eugene shook his head. "I didn't know him but the name sounds familiar."

"Are you sure?" I asked. "From what we've managed to find out, he was twenty-two years old and, as far as we can tell, had no reason for being here."

Eugene snorted. "If he was young and good-looking, that would have been enough of a reason."

Both Travis and I leaned forward. This sounded like it was going to be good.

"What do you mean by that?" Travis asked quietly.

Eugene looked uncertain, as though realizing that he may have said too much.

"It's okay," I said encouragingly.

Eugene didn't look to be convinced but he continued. "Back then this place was very different from what it is now. Miss Stanhope was the biggest star there was. Everyone knew her and everyone loved her. There were parties here all the time. Everyone who was anyone in this town came to those parties. It was the place to be if you wanted to be seen or discovered. This house would be full of all the hopefuls who would come to Hollywood looking to make their way. If you weren't rich and powerful, then you needed to be young and good-looking."

I frowned slightly. My impressions of Little Dottie did not include party animal, even less so now that I had met her and found her attached to a computer screen.

"Sounds like Dorothy Stanhope had some big ambitions," muttered Travis.

Eugene shook his head. "It wasn't Miss Stanhope," he said. "Miss Stanhope just did what her mother told her to do. Mrs Stanhope was the one with all the ambition. She was determined to make her daughter the biggest star in the world and she succeeded."

Travis and I exchanged glances. As long as there had been the movie industry there had been stage moms. I wasn't surprised to find that Little Dottie's mother had been one of them.

"Why didn't you tell us this while Martha was here?" I was curious. The information he had given us wasn't exactly earth-shattering. When he had walked back in here I had hoped that he had been planning to provide us with the murder weapon, or at least something equally as useful.

Eugene looked a little shame-faced. "Things were different back then. We were all young and sometimes things happen when you're young. Martha thinks that some things are better left in the past."

"Do you know who killed Giovanni Moretti?" I could hear the steel in Travis's voice.

Eugene shook his head. "No, but the fact that a body was found from that time doesn't surprise me at all."

"Why are you telling us this?" I asked.

From the moment I had entered this house, I had thought that Martha and Eugene were a single unit. I did not, for one moment, think that one of them would break ranks.

"You say that he has been in this house for the last sixty years. It explains a lot," Eugene said quietly. "There was a time when this house was filled with excitement and optimism. That ended about sixty years ago." Eugene looked me squarely in the face. "You say that you're a fan. Have you ever wondered why Miss Stanhope stopped making movies?"

I had always wondered that. "I assumed that she couldn't make the transition from child star to adult actress. It isn't exactly the first time that has happened."

"She could have made it," Eugene said confidently. "She was that talented. Something happened to her that changed her. It took any ambition that she might have had out of her."

"Her last movie was in the fifties," I murmured as I looked over at Travis who was watching the two of us.

Eugene nodded but didn't say anything else. He stood up. "I don't know who killed that man and I don't really care, but if it happened when you say it happened, it may have been the reason that all our lives ended up the way that they did."

We watched the stooped elderly man walk out of the room.

"That was interesting," said Travis.

And that was the understatement of the year. I was suspicious of the reasons that Eugene had decided to confide what he knew to us. I had trouble believing that it was for altruistic reasons. Since the moment I had walked into this house, I had seen Dorothy Stanhope, Martha and Eugene as an impenetrable fortress. I thought that it was only extreme loyalty that would have kept the three people together for so many years, and I had admired it. I rarely saw that loyalty in my working life and had thought it was something special. I was beginning to get the horrible feeling that there was a possibility that it might not be loyalty that was keeping these people together. Despite their protestations of not knowing who Giovanni Moretti was, I had a bad feeling that we were going to discover that the man had a bigger impact on their lives than they were letting on.

Chapter Eleven

"You ready to speak to the lady of the house?" Travis asked expectantly.

I shook my head. I did not want to speak to Dorothy Stanhope. This job had ended up being nothing like what I had hoped for when Monique had originally given me this assignment. I was getting a horrible feeling in the pit of my stomach that was telling me that it was only going to get worse.

"Too bad, it's your job now."

"Out of curiosity, why don't you have an assistant of your own?" I asked.

Travis grinned. "I haven't had time to organize one. Why? Are you looking for a career change?"

"I can quite honestly say that I don't think I am the kind of person who could work with you long-term," I said confidently. I had a feeling it would take someone with a lot more patience than I would ever possess to tolerate Travis Cooper and his ego on a daily basis.

"Your loss."

The sad thing was that I could tell that he really believed that.

Standing outside Dorothy Stanhope's office, I admitted to myself that I had mixed feelings to being a part of this interview. Two days before, I would have given anything to have one-on-one time with Dorothy Stanhope. Today, I wasn't so sure I wanted to know more about her.

Travis knocked heavily on the wooden door. It seemed that once they taught you that police knock, it never left you.

He glanced at me as we waited for an answer.

"Anything I should be aware of before we do this?"

I shrugged. "I barely met the woman. I don't think

she's very interested in people. She seems to be really into computer gaming, if that helps."

I could tell from the look on Travis's face that it didn't. He knocked again.

"You might want to just walk in. There is a very real possibility that she won't answer the door," I said sweetly.

"See, this is why I need an assistant. I would never have worked that out without you."

If I was honest with myself, I probably deserved the sarcasm.

Travis opened the door and I followed him into the darkened room. I could see the former actress hunched over at her desk, her eyes intent on the computer screen.

"Miss Stanhope?" I said quietly, hoping not to startle her.

"I don't think that's going to work," Travis muttered as he indicated the large gaming headphones that were perched precariously on the older woman's head.

There was no way that we were going to be subtle about this. I reached over and flicked the light switch on the wall. Dorothy screeched as the light flooded the room.

"What the…?"

She glared at us and Travis gave her his most winning smile.

"Do you know what you just did?"

"My name is Travis Cooper and you know Trudie Eyre."

I doubted very much that she remembered me, but there was a part of me that liked to believe that she did. The slight frown on the woman's face indicated that I was going to be disappointed.

"You just destroyed something that I have been working on for days."

Travis looked stunned. "You do realize that somebody has been killed on your property, don't you?" he asked.

Dorothy waved her hand in the air. "Martha said something about it. I've already spoken to the police and

Monique. I fail to see what it has to do with me."

I didn't even need to see the look on Travis's face to know his response to that statement.

"Monique Petit hired me to look into the case on your behalf. As part of that I need to speak to everyone who was living in this house sixty years ago. I understand that you lived in this house during the time period that the deceased met his end. As such I need to speak to you as well."

It was interesting to see that Travis was beginning to lose his legendary calm.

Dorothy looked petulant. I really should follow my own advice. If you admire someone, never work for them. It will inevitably cause them to crash down from whatever pedestal you put them on. I could also see that we needed to move the legendary Dorothy Stanhope away from the computer screen. I marveled at the fact that we were interviewing her about a murder which had taken place in her house while she was living there, and her eyes still kept wandering back to the screen.

"Maybe we should take a seat over there," I suggested, indicating the couches which were placed on the opposite side of the room from the computer.

"Very well." Dorothy Stanhope stalked over to the couches and dropped herself down.

Travis and I took the couch opposite and I waited for Travis to start.

"We believe that the body that Miss Eyre found in your attic has been there since early September in 1955."

"You are talking about a lifetime ago," Dorothy stated. "How can you expect me to remember anything from back then?"

"He has been identified as Giovanni Moretti…"

I nudged Travis to stop him. "Are you okay, Miss Stanhope?" I interrupted, concerned at the way the color had drained from the older woman's face.

"Are you sure that it's Johnny?"

I looked over at Travis and his face mirrored the confusion I felt. I got up and sat next to Dorothy, placing my hand on her arm and patting awkwardly.

"Who is Johnny?" I asked gently.

"Johnny Moretti. He was my boyfriend. He disappeared when I was eighteen." Her voice broke and she took in a shaky breath. "He left me a note saying that he couldn't handle the differences between us so he was leaving. I never saw him again."

"Differences?" I asked. "What kind of differences?"

Dorothy looked up at me and my heart broke at the misery in her eyes. "Johnny's family was very poor. He came from a bad area of the city, what we used to call the wrong side of the tracks. He'd left school early and worked in a garage. According to my mother, he was not the right sort of man for me to get involved with. We had to keep our relationship a secret." She drew in a shaky breath. "I loved him so much. It broke my heart when he left. I understood though. Everyone, on his side and mine, would point out how wrong we were for each other. He was very proud." She looked up at me. "He's really dead?"

I put my arm around her shoulder as I nodded and felt her crumple against me. I looked helplessly over at Travis as Dorothy Stanhope sobbed in my arms. There was nothing we could do. Though it looked like Johnny Moretti had died decades ago, the pain Dorothy was feeling was new and fresh. The three of us sat there while an old lady mourned a lost love. I could see that Travis was impatient with the situation but I glared at him over Dorothy's head, hoping that he understood that I was not going to let him badger the poor woman until she had dealt with the situation which had been put in front of her.

When I felt the shaking of her shoulders lessening, I nodded to Travis.

"Is there anything you can tell me from that time?" he asked gently. "We need to know everything that was happening when Johnny died."

Dorothy sniffed loudly as she sat back up and pulled away from me. I reached into my bag to find a tissue and passed it to her. She blew her nose noisily.

"I was eighteen when I met Johnny. He worked in a local gas station. I had just bought my first car. My mother wasn't too happy about me having a car. She thought it was dangerous. I just loved the freedom. Since I was a child I always had someone looking over my shoulder, making sure that I was doing the right thing in the right way. Having that car meant I could go anywhere I wanted and, more importantly, I could go alone. I was never alone."

In that moment I felt so sorry for Dorothy. To want something so basic as to having some time to yourself, and never being able to get it, was sad.

Dorothy smiled. "I remember getting that car and everyone saying that Martin needed to go with me for that first drive."

"Martin Harrington?" Travis interrupted.

I couldn't quite interpret the look on Dorothy's face, but it was a safe bet that it wasn't caused by a pleasant memory.

"Yes," she said hurriedly. "Martin's family and my family had known each other for years. We had pretty much grown up together." Dorothy looked up sadly. "Everyone expected us to get married, including Martin."

"But not you," I commented.

Dorothy shrugged. "I didn't know at that stage. I was young and didn't know anything about love. Martin was handsome and came from a good family. Mother said he had real prospects. It seemed as good a choice as any."

Dorothy's eyes seemed to glaze over as she got lost in her memories. "I picked up my car, went for a long drive and nearly ran out of gas. I found out later that someone had ensured that the tank was almost empty. I always thought that Martin wanted me to get stuck and get a bit of a scare so I would learn a lesson."

The more I heard about Martin Harrington, the more I realized that I should really trust my instincts more.

"I barely made it to the gas station. I was feeling a little silly when Johnny filled up the tank. He was so sweet to me. I ended up going to that gas station all the time." She laughed softly. "Even when the tank was only half empty. He showed me how to do things on my car like check the oil and change a tire. He treated me like I was a normal person." Dorothy stopped talking for a moment and looked at us. "Do you know how wonderful that was for me? He treated me like I was capable. Everyone else looked at me as this trophy thing that you pulled out to perform and then put away. Everything was taken care of by staff or the studio. I wasn't supposed to have an independent thought in my head. And there was Johnny, who believed that I could do anything that I set my mind to. We started dating. We had to do it quietly so nobody would know what was happening. Nobody in my life would have approved. They were already mapping out the rest of my life without my input. The last thing they wanted was for me to actually start thinking for myself."

Dorothy smiled softly. "I thought we were going to get married. I wanted so much to be his wife. Then I got the letter. He said that he didn't want to ruin my future. Our lives were too different. I never saw him again. I assumed that he started his own life away from me. It broke my heart."

"Do you still have that note?" Travis asked.

Dorothy stood up and walked over to a set of drawers at the side of the room. Opening the top one, she pulled out a piece of paper.

"Here it is," she said as she passed it to Travis.

It said a lot that even after sixty years she knew exactly where to find that letter. I had a feeling that she still read it often.

I watched as Travis read the letter, and I liked to think that even his jaded heart was touched by Dorothy's story.

"I'd like to take this letter and see if I can get it authenticated."

I could see Dorothy hesitating at Travis's request. Considering how affected she still seemed to be by the letter, I was surprised that she had even let Travis read it.

"We'll make sure you get it back," I assured her.

"Very well," Dorothy agreed. "Please make sure that it isn't damaged. Now that I know that he is really gone, it is all that I have left of him." She hesitated for a moment. "You are sure it is him, aren't you?"

"As sure as we can be," I said. "The body was found with his wallet and dental records confirmed the identification."

Dorothy's eyes filled with tears again. "I don't understand. He was the sweetest and gentlest person you could possibly know. Why would anyone want to kill him?"

"I think the question is more, why was he killed in this house?"

I could see that Dorothy was startled by Travis's question.

"What are you talking about? No person in this house would ever hurt Johnny."

"Are you sure?" Travis persisted. "You just said that you hid the relationship because you were afraid of the way the people in your life would react."

"But they wouldn't have killed him," Dorothy maintained. "He had left me anyway. There was no reason for anyone to kill him."

"Did he talk about anyone in his life that may have wished him harm?" I asked gently.

Dorothy started to shake her head, but then stopped as if a stray thought had hit her.

"Johnny didn't talk about his life much. I don't think he wanted to remind me of the differences in our lives. I do remember we once ran into a couple of friends of his when we were out together. He seemed to want to get me away from them as quickly as possible. When I asked him about it, he said that he didn't want me exposed to some of the darker parts of his world."

Travis and I exchanged glances. "Do you by any chance remember who these people were and why Johnny was worried about them?" Travis asked.

"He never spoke about them. I could tell that he was uncomfortable with the whole situation so I didn't ask." Dorothy dropped her head. "I wish I'd asked. Maybe I could have done something to help him. He was so proud." Dorothy looked up at me, her eyes shining. "I would have done anything for him. He was the only part of my life that made me feel happy."

I smiled weakly at her. For the first time since I'd met her, Dorothy Stanhope seemed to be a real person. She was no longer the unrealistic larger than life character from my childhood, or the crushing disappointment that I had been dealing with the last two days. She was a woman who had loved and lost, someone I could relate to very well.

"Is there anything I can do for you?" I murmured, wondering if there was any way that I could make this situation better.

Dorothy looked up and shook her head. "Just find out what happened to him," she said as the tears glistened in her eyes. "He was a good person. It shouldn't have happened to him."

I nodded quickly and stood up. Dorothy grabbed my hand and prevented my moving away from her. "Are you going to speak to his family?"

I looked over at Travis and he nodded.

I patted her hand awkwardly. "We'll be talking to everyone that we can find."

"Tell them I loved him."

"I'll do that."

Dorothy smiled gratefully as she clasped her hands in her lap. "Thank you. I just want them to know how special he was."

I didn't say a word to Travis as we walked out of the office. As I softly closed the door I saw Dorothy gazing across the room at nothing in particular, lost in a world of memories.

Chapter Twelve

"What's next?" I asked, still feeling some of the emotion of the interview with Dorothy Stanhope.

"I'm hungry. I think we'll grab some lunch."

Travis was obviously less affected. I can't say that surprised me.

Sitting across from Travis in a diner as he inhaled a burger, I marveled at his ability to not be affected by Dorothy's story. Although, considering his line of work, if he was affected by every heartbreak story he heard, I could not see him functioning at all.

As I reluctantly picked at the food on my plate I glanced down at my phone for what felt like the hundredth time.

"You know that could be construed as being very rude," Travis remarked.

"What do you mean?" I asked, almost pleased that Travis had decided to kindly present himself as a target for my current irritability.

"You keep glancing at your phone while you and I are supposed to be having a pleasant lunch together."

"It's a burger and fries," I said dryly.

"It's a sit down meal with me. Usually I have no problem keeping a woman's attention during a date."

"This is not a date. If you ever call it that again I will make sure that your life is no longer worth living," I warned. The last thing I needed was for Travis to casually drop into a conversation with Griffin that he and I had gone out on a date. Unfortunately, that was just the sort of thing that he would ensure he did at the earliest opportunity.

"You waiting for a call?" Travis queried.

I shook my head. "No, I just don't want to miss one if it comes in."

"You and Griffin have an argument?"

"Of course not."

Travis chuckled. "Then things must be really bad if you're not even arguing about whatever is wrong with you at the moment."

"Nothing's wrong." I frowned as I could hear the uncertainty in my own voice.

Travis leaned back. "Has anyone ever told you that you are the worst liar ever?"

I stayed silent. I already knew that my ability to lie was pretty much non-existent. I didn't feel the need to prove Travis's point for him.

"Talk to Uncle Travis, tell me what's going on. You'll feel better."

I doubted that very much, but I was feeling weak. There was no other reason for me to discuss my personal life with the man who took great pleasure in making fun of it.

"My ex-fiancé turned up yesterday," I blurted out, knowing that I was definitely going to regret doing it.

"I already know your ex-fiancé turned up."

Travis looked slightly bored, and at that point I realized that there was no point in backing out now.

"He flew over from Australia to tell me he still loved me, and then he told Griffin that he was just a rebound guy."

There was silence and I was a bit concerned that I was going to need to repeat myself.

"Does your ex have a death wish?" Travis asked conversationally.

"Of course not. He just doesn't really think things through before doing them."

"Obviously not." Travis put down his fries and looked me directly in the eyes. "Do you still love him?"

I paused for a moment, surprised by the serious

expression on Travis's face. "No, I don't love him anymore. There is a part of me that has some nostalgia for what we used to have, but it's tied up with how sometimes I get homesick. I still wouldn't trade what I have now with Griffin for what I had then with Paul."

Travis watched me for a moment as if trying to satisfy himself that I was being honest with him and myself. "You need to tell Griffin that and you need to tell Paul that. The worst possible thing you can do to either of them is to leave them in any doubt about how you feel."

"I am shocked at how good that advice is," I said as I watched Travis pick up some fries and resume eating.

Travis raised an eyebrow. "With all my experience dealing with the worst kinds of relationships, I've picked up a few skills here and there."

"Just unable to apply it to your own life," I pointed out.

"I'm doing fine," Travis protested.

"Sure you are. I just have one question for you. How many women have you gone out with just once?"

Travis stopped and looked around the diner thoughtfully. "Pretty much all of them."

My jaw dropped. "You're telling me that you only go out with a woman once?"

Travis nodded, looking slightly discomfited by my appraisal.

"You are so much more damaged than I originally thought."

Travis grimaced. "Please don't tell me that you think that I need the love of a good woman."

I smiled angelically. "It hasn't hurt Griffin. He seems happy."

Travis looked at me. "Griffin is having to deal with your ex. I can pretty much guarantee that the last thing he is feeling at the moment is happy."

"This is just a tiny bump in the road," I protested. "It doesn't mean anything and it will blow over in no time at all."

Travis shook his head. "I've seen this kind of thing plenty of times before. Guy gets involved young, stays with the same girl for years. All of a sudden something happens and he panics. Decides he wants to sow his wild oats. He's always got it in the back of his mind that maybe, just maybe, he didn't make quite the right decision, but he's having too much fun to really think about it. Then he finds out that the girl, the one he's always thought he was going to end up with, has another guy sniffing after her. All of a sudden she's the love of his life and he can't imagine his future without her. He's come to sabotage the wedding and because you were with him so long, he knows exactly how to go about doing that in the most effective way possible."

"I thought you said all I needed to do was tell him how I really felt and it would all be fine."

Travis smiled. "I gave a suggestion. I have no idea if it is going to work."

"That is not comforting."

Travis grinned. "You lost the right to get comforting from me when you said I was damaged."

"Any woman who can put up with you for any length of time would have to be a saint, and if you find her, I would really like to meet her."

"So would I," murmured Travis.

I watched him curiously, surprised by that statement. Before I could say anything Travis stood up abruptly.

"We need to speak to Moretti's sister."

I grabbed my purse and phone and followed him out of the diner. "She's still around?" I asked, surprised by both the news that Travis had been able to track down Johnny Moretti's family and the way he seemed to be running from our conversation.

"She's in a nursing home. According to the information that I was able to find out about Johnny Moretti she is the only surviving family."

As we settled into Travis's car, a horrible thought

occurred to me. "Please tell me someone has notified her that her brother's body has been found." I really didn't want to have to be part of a death notification. The last time I did that with Travis, it had not ended well. To be more accurate it had ended with Travis's car being destroyed with a baseball bat. Not an experience that I was keen on repeating.

Travis smiled tightly. "One of my contacts in the department sent me a message that they had notified her."

"Griffin?" I asked hopefully.

"The day that man willingly gives me information will be the day I start worrying," Travis said gravely.

He was right. Travis and Griffin had a complicated relationship. I usually tried my best not to get in the middle of it. To be perfectly honest, I usually failed.

Chapter Thirteen

Once again Travis and I were sitting across from a woman with tears in her eyes about a death that happened sixty years ago.

"I knew Johnny getting involved with that woman was a bad idea. The people around her were never going to let him have her. She was their meal ticket. They were never going to let her go."

I nodded sympathetically. As usual the protective sister had called it.

"I wish he'd never met those people."

"My understanding is that Dorothy Stanhope really cared about your brother." I hoped that piece of information would lessen some of the pain that Rosa Moretti was feeling.

"She may have loved him but I don't think he felt the same way about her."

I was pretty sure that the confusion on Travis's face was mirrored on mine.

"What do you mean by that?" Travis asked slowly.

A part of me didn't want to hear the answer.

"I knew my brother and I could always tell when he was in love." Rosa smiled slightly at the memory. "I don't know why he got involved with Dorothy Stanhope, but he did not love her."

Travis stood up and started pacing. "Okay, we're going to need to back up a little bit. The information we received was that your brother was secretly dating Dorothy Stanhope against the wishes of her family." Travis fished into his pocket and pulled out the letter that Dorothy had given him. "He sent this letter breaking up with her just before he died."

Rosa read through it. "That's his writing but I'm not

entirely sure that those are his feelings or even his words."

My stomach plummeted. There are few people I dislike more than those that manipulate other people's emotions for their own twisted reasons. I really hoped that Rosa was wrong about her brother.

"Are you able to help us understand what is going on here?" I asked gently. "We only started looking into your brother's death today. So far, all we know is that Dorothy Stanhope was madly in love with your brother, and she believed that he truly loved her too."

For the first time I could see sympathy in Rosa's eyes. "Johnny wasn't a bad person. He just sometimes got into situations that spiraled out of control. When he fell for a woman, he fell hard. He was a good-looking guy and he could use that to get ahead. He might have been fond of Dorothy Stanhope. Who knows, given time, he might have even fallen in love with her. But I do know that his getting involved with her was not an accident."

"Was there anyone else from that time who would have more information?" Travis asked, his face drawn in a frown. It looked like he found the current turn of events as distasteful as I did.

"I don't know. It was so long ago." She closed her eyes. "I'm tired. I need you to go now."

It was obvious we weren't going to get anything more out of her. Travis and I walked quietly to the car and I noticed Travis watching me.

"Don't say it," I mumbled.

"Don't say what?"

"It just seems that whenever I'm around you, I always get the chance to see the worst that relationships have to offer."

Travis grinned wryly. "Comes with the job. Nice, healthy relationships have a tendency not to cross my path."

"No wonder you're so messed up."

"No wonder," Travis repeated quietly.

I glanced over at Travis. Usually at this point he was reveling in my naive optimism about love. Today he seemed to be as demoralized by what was happening as I was.

"You okay?" I queried.

The smile Travis gave me seemed a bit forced but it was back. "Of course I'm okay."

As we drove back to Dorothy Stanhope's house, it surprised me that at the end of what had been a truly dissatisfying day, my overriding emotion was concern for Travis Cooper. I was almost horrified by the realization that I was becoming quite fond of Travis. This had definitely been one of my stranger days.

My musings were interrupted when my phone started ringing. Scrambling in my bag I hoped that it was Griffin calling me.

I don't think I was understating my disappointment when I heard Monique's voice.

"Oh, it's you."

Monique paused as I was pretty sure that wasn't how she was used to being greeted.

"Did you wish to explain your lack of enthusiasm, ma petite?"

I grimaced. "Not particularly." I really did not want to explain what was going on in my life with Monique. She probably already knew everything that was happening, including the knot that was growing in my stomach the longer I was going without hearing from Griffin.

"What can I do for you?"

I waited as Monique decided whether to pursue me on why she deserved my less than enthusiastic greeting.

"I've just been contacted by your client."

I let out the tense breath that I had been holding in. It looked like we were going to ignore my stunningly bad move. I was sure we'd get back to it at a later time though.

"You have been asked to organize the funeral."

I should have expected that, but a part of me was

concerned that Dorothy was being a bit high-handed.

"Has it been cleared with the family?" I queried.

"Yes, my understanding is that the sister is not in much of a position to organize anything. She was relieved that you will be doing it."

"Of course," I murmured.

I hung up and found Travis glancing over at me with a concerned look on his face.

"What's wrong?"

I forced a smile. "Nothing much. This situation just seems to be a little unsettling."

"How so? Other than the fact we're looking for a killer from about sixty years ago."

"That's just it. Because it happened so long ago there just seems to be this huge disconnect. I've just been told that I'm organizing the funeral on Dorothy Stanhope's orders. If the murder had happened a day ago rather than sixty years ago, I don't think everyone would be quite so happy that the owner of the house where the body was found would be the one taking care of the funeral arrangements."

Travis shrugged. "Seems logical to me. That nursing home didn't leave me with any confidence that Johnny's sister had much in the way of money, and I can't find any other family. Dorothy Stanhope is the one person who seems to be able to afford the funeral. The sister is probably glad that she doesn't have to worry about it."

"I guess so," I murmured. "But Dorothy doesn't seem to have much in the way of money either. I mean, that's how this mess started, isn't it? I was brought in to start sorting out her old stuff so that it could be sold because she needed money to renovate that house of hers."

"She would have to have money somewhere," Travis pointed out. "I know she hasn't worked for decades but she has had some serious money. I know Martin Harrington's father was the one who took care of things for her financially years ago. He had a lot of clients from that era. Everyone knew he had a gift for making his clients very rich. Dorothy Stanhope was always at the top of that pile."

"Maybe she lost the money in bad investments."

"Maybe," Travis said thoughtfully. "Maybe she has a hidden vice that we don't know about. Something that she's poured her money into all these years."

I could see why Travis would immediately go for the worst case scenario. I had trouble seeing it. The Dorothy Stanhope that I had met didn't strike me as being a tormented artist who had poured her fortune into the bottom of a spirits glass as so many had done before her. To me she seemed sad. Like she had lost a vital spark of herself at some point and had no way of getting it back. I grimaced at the way my mind was going. To distract myself I called Tomas Burnelli, funeral planner to the stars.

"Hi Trudie, how's my favorite repeat customer?"

That was harsh. I didn't think I'd been required to use Tomas's services as often as he felt I did.

"Hi Tomas. Can we meet up for a coffee?"

"Just for coffee?" Tomas queried, sounding a little disappointed. "You don't want to shove me in a closet to avoid a muscle-bound thug threatening somebody?"

"Not today."

"So disappointing," he murmured.

I very quickly organized a time to meet after work and hung up the phone.

"Looks like you're in for a fun evening," Travis commented.

I grimaced. Don't get me wrong, I adored Tomas. If you had to spend time with a funeral planner, he was definitely the one you would want to have a coffee with. Of course, meeting with him let me put off going home to what I assumed was going to be an empty apartment. So that would be a benefit. Nothing like avoiding an unpleasant situation. Though what that said about me was something I wasn't really very interested in exploring.

"You're not a coward."

I spun my head to the side. "How on Earth did you know what I was thinking?"

Travis rolled his eyes. "I wish you would remember that I am a fully trained detective. I can read people like a book. Also, you have one of those faces where everything you are thinking is written plainly on your face. It's almost embarrassingly easy to work out what you are thinking about."

Just what I needed to know, not that it was any great surprise to me. It was one of the reasons I was a hopeless liar. I still maintained that was a good thing despite some of my friends stating otherwise.

When we pulled up at the Stanhope mansion I turned to Travis. "You coming in?"

"No," Travis said quietly. "I've got a feeling that there is something else going on here that we are missing. I think we're only being given a small part of the picture and I need to look into some other areas."

I waited for him to explain but it looked like he wasn't in a sharing mood.

"Okay. I'll see you tomorrow then."

Travis nodded sharply and I watched as his car peeled away from the property.

"Friend of yours?"

I gasped and spun around to find Eugene standing behind me.

"Don't do that. You scared the living daylights out of me."

Eugene smiled sheepishly. "Sorry about that. I've spent so many years working alone in these gardens that I sometimes forget how to act around people."

I looked at him curiously. There seemed to have been a shift in the way Eugene was speaking to me. I no longer appeared to be the interloper who was disrupting their lives. Considering how much I had disrupted their lives in the less than forty-eight hours I had been there, I found this change of attitude to be refreshing and a little concerning.

"Anything interesting happen while I've been away?"

Eugene smiled and it lit up his face in a way that I hadn't seen before. "Dorothy's outside, walking through the garden."

"Really?" From the little I had seen of Dorothy Stanhope I thought it was going to take something major to remove her from behind her computer.

"She hasn't done that in years," Eugene continued. "She said the roses were lovely."

I smiled at the amount of pride I was hearing in Eugene's voice and looked over his shoulder. Sure enough, there was Dorothy wandering through the gardens, looking as if she hadn't seen them in years.

I left Eugene and walked over to her. "They are lovely, aren't they?" I commented as I watched her touch the delicate petals of a rose.

Dorothy looked startled at my approach. "Yes, they are. I haven't been out here for a while. Eugene's done a lovely job, hasn't he?"

"He does seem to have the gift," I murmured. There was no doubt that the gardens were not immaculate. There was too much work for just one man. But you could see the love and attention that one man put into the gardens and it seemed he had focused on what he thought were the important areas.

"I simply love roses." Dorothy smiled up at me as she breathed in the scent of a beautiful pink specimen. "I always have."

It looked like Eugene knew his audience well. I hated to do something which I knew would disturb the sense of peace I could see that Dorothy had found while walking among the flowers.

"Monique contacted me about Johnny Moretti's funeral."

Just as I had expected, the peaceful expression on

Dorothy's face disappeared.

"Yes, I think it's important that he have a proper send off. The idea of him in my attic for the last sixty years makes me sick. The least I can do is make sure he gets treated with dignity now."

Dorothy seemed sincere in what she was saying, but there was just a part of this that made me feel slightly uncomfortable. "Does his family want anything to do with the funeral?"

Dorothy shook her head. "Monique spoke to his sister. She can't even afford to claim his body. If I don't do it his body may stay unclaimed for years. Sixty years ago I loved him with all my heart. I can't allow that to happen."

I nodded sharply. I understood. Sometimes we do what we have to.

"I'll start organizing it immediately. I have a meeting with the funeral planner this afternoon. Is there anything special that I need to be aware of?"

Dorothy shook her head. "No, I just think it needs to be done as simply and quickly as possible."

"I'll make sure it's done. I'll see you tomorrow. Enjoy your garden."

Dorothy smiled tentatively and I walked away. Before I got in my car I looked back to see that Eugene had joined Dorothy. She was talking animatedly while pointing towards some of the flowers. For the first time this place seemed normal, as if removing the body of Johnny Moretti had lifted a darkness from the house. I shivered despite the warmth of the afternoon sun.

Chapter Fourteen

As I waited for Tomas at the coffee shop, I wondered about the concept of curses. When I had walked into the Stanhope house there had seemed to be an oppressiveness in the air. The people had seemed worn down by it. With Johnny's body gone, there seemed to be a lightness entering the people as if the discovery of his body had brought an end to something. What that something was, I didn't know yet. But I had a feeling that it was going to be important that we find out. I just hoped it didn't bring back the darkness.

My musings were interrupted when arms were flung around my shoulders and I was captured in a heartfelt hug.

"Trudie, it is so good to see you."

Tomas Burnelli was one of the most effervescent human beings that I knew. It seemed strange that he also had a reputation as being one of the best funeral planners in Los Angeles. He let go of me and dropped himself into the chair opposite.

"What can I do for you today?" Tomas gasped and grabbed my left hand. "You're engaged. Congratulations!"

He held my hand up to the light and studied the diamond ring intently. "It's small but very good quality."

I snatched my hand back. "Stop critiquing my ring. I love it." I also knew from my future father-in-law that Griffin had agonized over getting just the right ring for me.

Tomas smiled. "I wasn't being critical. It's nice to see someone who doesn't need to have a ten pound ring to flash around to prove their love." He went to have a sip of his coffee when he froze, a horrible thought obviously crossing his mind. "Are you going to ask me to organize your wedding?"

There was a part of me that was tempted to do just that. The man had, before becoming a funeral events planner, been a wedding planner. Of course, that was before he had developed an almost pathological aversion to all things bridal. I could tell that if I asked him to plan my wedding we would be stretching the friendship maybe a little too far. I waited a few seconds before answering. It was always entertaining in these circumstances to prolong the agony.

"No."

Tomas exhaled noisily.

"I'll organize my own wedding, thank you very much. I asked you here for a different reason. I have a client who has asked me to organize a funeral for them. Very small, very low key."

"No bigamy, no extortion?"

I did not appreciate the eagerness in his voice.

"Nothing like that." I really hoped nothing like that would be coming up at Johnny Moretti's funeral.

"So disappointing," Tomas sighed, although he had a twinkle in his eye. Which showed he still hoped for something special.

Tomas pulled out his trusty notebook and started writing.

"Name?"

"Giovanni Moretti, but everybody seems to have called him Johnny."

"Method of death?"

"Looks like he had the back of his head bashed in." I lowered my voice when I noticed that people at the next table were watching us curiously. If I overheard this conversation I would have been concerned too.

"That shouldn't be a problem for Helena."

Usually I would have agreed with Tomas. Helena was his favorite cosmetician and I had used her on occasion. She was truly gifted, making the dead look alive and covering up violent deaths in a way that bordered on supernatural. She was also a little eccentric but her skill made that easy to overlook. I had my doubts whether her talents extended as far as they would be needed for this case.

"Not even Helena could do anything with this guy. He was found mummified in a trunk in an attic. It looks like he'd been there for sixty years." Despite the warmth of the day I felt a shiver go through me at the memory of opening that trunk. I seemed to be doing that a lot today.

"You found him didn't you?"

"For a funeral planner you have an entirely too gleeful look on your face."

"You found him."

"Fine, I found him. Can we please move on?"

"Are you absolutely sure Helena can't work on him? She did wonders for that guy with the bullet hole in his head that you brought us."

The people at the table next to us got up abruptly and moved to a table outside. I almost felt like I should apologize.

"You're scaring people," I pointed out to Tomas. "And I've got to admit, you're starting to scare me."

He sighed dramatically. "Closed casket it is then. How many people?"

I had absolutely no idea. "Ten."

"That was a guess, wasn't it? You don't have a clue how many people are going to turn up."

"Can't get anything past you, can I?"

Tomas sighed again. "I know the perfect place. It's small enough to be intimate but if more people turn up we can cater for that as well."

"I knew I could count on you."

"I feel like I'm being taken advantage of."

"I could be asking you to organize my wedding."

That panicked look returned to Tomas's face. "Point taken."

I thought it would be.

Chapter Fifteen

As I drove home I thought about Tomas and his aversion to weddings. I couldn't say that I didn't understand it. I had been loath to get started on the planning of my own wedding. I'd seen too many over-the-top celebrations where family strife had been the theme of the day. I squelched the errant insecure thought that at this moment I wasn't entirely sure whether a wedding would be happening. I couldn't help the sigh of relief when I reached my apartment building and saw Griffin's truck in the parking lot. I sat in my car for a moment, gathering my thoughts before heading to my apartment. I knew that how we dealt with the Paul situation was going to be important to the future of our relationship. I really didn't want to mess it up.

The apartment was quiet when I walked in and I found Griffin sitting on the couch, waiting for me. I dropped my purse on the side table and sat down opposite him.

"You're back." I was always impressed with my ability to state the obvious.

"Yeah, I shouldn't have taken off like that. I'm sorry."

This couldn't be good. We were only seconds into the conversation and I already received an apology. "Not exactly one of your finer moments."

Griffin grimaced. "Your ex managed to get under my skin."

"That was always Paul's specialty."

"I was angry and I didn't want to direct any of it at you because I know this isn't your fault."

This discussion was going so much better than our arguments usually went. I usually had to defend myself, Griffin rarely jumped in and did it for me.

"I don't like the fact he is here," I said quietly. "I have had no contact with him since I was in hospital. I don't want him here and I don't have any interest in anything that he has to say. I don't know how to make it clearer than that. I'm not sure what he said to you, but it makes no difference to me and to what we have between us."

Griffin stood up and pulled me into his arms. "I know that, it was just good to hear you say it."

The knot that had taken residence in my stomach for the last twenty-four hours started to loosen as I nestled against his chest.

"While you're feeling guilty there's something that I need to tell you."

"That doesn't sound good."

Griffin was right but I needed to tell him. There was no way that I was going to keep the details of my latest job from him. I had learned my lesson about that from a previous assignment. I like to think that I am able to learn from my past mistakes.

"I'm working with Travis."

The arms wrapped around me tightened momentarily.

"You're what?"

"Travis has been hired to look into the Johnny Moretti case because the police don't seem to be interested. I've been roped into being his assistant."

"You're working for Travis Cooper?"

"I really wish I wasn't."

As the silence dragged on I looked up into Griffin's face.

"Are you okay?" Griffin looked concerned, but at this moment it was far less sympathy than I felt I deserved.

"No, I'm not okay. As of today I am working for Travis Cooper in investigating the case of the mummified body in the attic. And let me tell you, that man is driving me nuts. I don't know how you kept up with him as long as you did. I am so sorry for severely underestimating your level of patience."

I could tell from the expression on Griffin's face that he had no idea how to deal with that statement. On one hand, I knew that he wouldn't be happy with the fact that I was working for Travis. On the other, I had finally acknowledged what he had been saying about Travis Cooper for ages, that the man may be charming but he was a lot of work.

"I guess there could be worse people for you to work with."

I almost choked. The world had indeed turned if Griffin was that okay with me working with Travis.

Hearing a knock at the door, I pulled away from Griffin.

"I'll get it. Crystal probably saw me get home and waited what she thought was an appropriate amount of time before coming over."

"I don't think we have the same interpretation of the term appropriate."

Despite the gruffness in his tone I knew that Griffin was fond of Crystal. At least most days he was.

Opening my front door, I realized that what I had expected to happen since the moment I had seen Paul had come to pass. My family lived in a pretty small farming community in rural Australia. When Paul dumped me the people of the town developed some pretty strong opinions on his actions and the rightness of them. Even if he had tried to keep quiet about his trip to LA to sabotage my relationship, someone, somewhere, would have found out. Through the community grapevine that information would have found its way to my family's kitchen table where a council of war would be called. During that meeting it would have been discussed which member of my family should fly up here, which of them had the tactical ability to protect me while also having the compassion to deal with any emotional fallout when I was presented with the specter of my old relationship. I know that is what had happened because I know my family. What I failed to understand was why after what was surely a long and carefully considered discussion it was my Grandma Rita who had been chosen to be the superhero to swoop in and save me. Admittedly, the woman during a certain period of her life had taken to wearing a cape. There was also that one occasion when she got into the sherry and wore her underwear on the outside of her clothes. Despite that, I was sure that there would have been a better choice for the job.

I immediately slammed the door shut.

"What are you doing?"

It seemed Griffin no longer felt confident in allowing me to answer the door on my own and had followed me.

"I don't know."

"Who was that?"

"My grandmother."

Griffin eyed me incredulously. "When your ex-fiancé turned up you stood there with the door wide open. Your grandmother turns up and you slam the door in her face. Is there a reason that the woman who probably loves you deserves that kind of treatment?"

I shrugged helplessly. I no longer seemed to be in control of my actions.

Griffin leaned over and opened the door to my grandmother, who didn't look nearly as annoyed as I expected her to be.

"I am so sorry," he said. "We're not really sure why that happened."

Grandma Rita picked up her bag and entered the apartment. "Not the first time I've had a door slammed in my face. Her mother does it to me all the time."

Grandma Rita put down her bag and looked Griffin up and down while ignoring me completely.

"So you're the one that my daughter-in-law doesn't think is good enough for her little girl."

Inwardly I groaned. I really wished that my mother could get past her first impressions of Griffin.

My grandmother grinned as she wrapped her arms around a stunned and clearly disturbed Griffin. "That's a good enough reason for me to like you, my boy."

Of course, I should have realized that my mother's disdain was guaranteed to ensure that my Grandma Rita was going to adore Griffin, if only to annoy the hell out of her least favorite daughter-in-law.

Griffin patted my small grandmother awkwardly on the back. I appreciated the time he was giving me to wrap my head around the latest development in the saga that was my life. I could have told him that no amount of time was going to help me prepare for what this woman had in store for me.

Eventually, the pleading look on my fiancé's face to rescue him was too much. I cleared my throat. "Grandma Rita, what are you doing here?"

Reluctantly the older woman let go of Griffin.

"I believe you have a problem."

I had several problems, not the least of which was the mummified body of Johnny Moretti. I was, however, assuming that she meant the 'Paul situation'.

"I'm dealing with it."

"Probably very badly."

It was good to see the confidence my own grandmother had in me.

"I've told him to go away," I said tiredly.

Grandma Rita snorted indelicately. "I'm assuming that went as well as I think it would."

I grimaced. "You know Paul."

"I did like that boy," she said sadly. "I never expected things to work out the way that they did."

I didn't like the way this conversation was going. My whole family had adored Paul, but things changed. I glanced over at Griffin to see that he had that uncomfortable look on his face again. That was unfortunate as I was about to make his night worse.

"How long are you staying, Grandma?"

"As long as I'm needed."

Oh, this was just getting better and better.

"I'll set up your room."

I knew how cowardly it was of me to escape, but this wasn't how things were supposed to happen. My family was only supposed to find out about this situation after I had solved it and Paul had left, never to enter my life again.

I looked up as Griffin entered the room, closing the door behind him.

"Nice of you to leave me out there with her."

I dropped my head. "I'm sorry." I had a sudden thought. "You left her out there alone. Are you nuts? She'll be going through our bedside tables before you can blink."

Griffin put up my hands to stop me preventing my grandmother from having even more humiliating information on me than she previously had.

"She's fine. Miss Betsy, Sean and Crystal came by. They're entertaining her as we speak. Or more accurately, she's entertaining them with stories from your childhood. Did you really hop on an ATV and drive it straight into a concrete wall?"

I grimaced. "We call them quad bikes and yes, I did. But I only did it because Paul dared me to. The concrete wall part was an accident."

"He figures a lot in your stories, doesn't he?"

I nodded as I sat down heavily on the bed.

"Is that why you don't tell me things from your past?"

I couldn't stop the sigh that escaped me. "Most of my childhood stories through to my early twenties have Paul as a supporting character. When our relationship ended it was just easier to put everything in a little box in my mind and leave it there. I didn't want to tell you those stories because I didn't think you'd appreciate the constant reminders of my ex."

Griffin sat down next to me. "I want to hear about the stupid things you did as a kid. I'll deal with the part he played in them."

I gave him a fierce hug and held on tight. "I love you."

"I love you too. Now, are you ready to face what is happening out there, or are you planning on hiding in here for the rest of the night?"

I knew which option I wanted to take. I also knew which option I had to take. "I'll go out there."

"I'll be right behind you."

I did note that Griffin hadn't offered to be first out the door.

I shouldn't have been surprised to find that Edwin had joined the group, especially as he'd brought food. I loved how my friends believed that the way to show love and support always involved pizza and ice cream. I was surprised to find Lee had arrived and was currently cornered by my grandmother. The desperate look in his eyes was one that I knew only too well. I elbowed my grandmother out of the way as I gave Lee a hug.

"It's good to see you, Lee."

As he leaned over me I heard him frantically whisper in my ear. "Help me."

I wasn't surprised to learn that my grandmother was capable of reducing a tough ex-cop to this state of fear.

"Grandma." I turned around, making sure that I kept Lee behind me. "Please stop scaring my future father-in-law."

I could feel Lee groan behind me. If he was looking for subtle he was looking at the wrong family.

To prove my point Grandma Rita pouted. "But it's so much fun when they get that panicked look on their face."

Of course it was. Grandma Rita always enjoyed torturing future members of the Eyre family. It was why she and my mother had such a volatile relationship.

"I thought you were here to rescue me, not torture the men of the Griffin family."

My small delicate grandmother grabbed a large slice of pizza. "You know me, my darling angel. I'm perfectly capable of doing both."

As well as committing several felonies along the way. My grandmother specialized at multitasking.

She chewed thoughtfully on her pizza. "So what are you going to do?"

The room went silent as everyone waited for me to answer her. I looked around at the people who loved me enough to view this mess in my personal life as something that needed to be solved quickly so I could move forward with Griffin. As I looked around, the one person I focused on was Lee. Unlike everyone else, he wasn't watching me. He was watching his son, the concern written all over his face. I had to fix this. I made a decision. I was over Paul causing this much disruption in my life.

"I'm going to meet with him," I said quietly. Obviously not quietly enough because the response was instantaneous.

"What did you say?" asked Crystal.

"I'm done with having this hanging over my head. I need to get this situation sorted out and the best way to do that is to let him have his say."

"So you're going to meet him for what…a date?" I could almost see the hurt in Griffin's eyes.

"I will meet him for a coffee, and Edwin will be coming with me."

Edwin looked up, almost choking on a mouth full of pizza.

"Why me?" he asked once his throat was cleared.

"Because I know that no one in this room wants me to go alone, but everyone here is a little on edge about the situation. Out of everyone here you are the least likely to do or say anything to make things worse."

I raised an eyebrow in challenge to the rest of the group to refute my statement. They couldn't. It went without saying that Griffin and Grandma Rita were out. There was no way I could have a conversation with Paul with either of them in hearing distance. I wouldn't put it past Crystal, Miss Betsy and Sean to organize an unpleasant accident to befall Paul if they were involved. Lee may have been a choice because he came across as one of the more level-headed people of my acquaintance, but I still had a feeling that keeping his silence was going to be a step too far for him. No, Edwin was the best choice, if only for the fact I had a half decent chance of controlling his reactions to anything that Paul said.

"I think that's a good idea."

Despite her faults I could always depend on Grandma Rita to back me up. Of course, she would have said the same thing if I had proposed killing Paul and dumping his body across the border. She was that kind of grandmother.

The room went silent and I could see all the worried glances that were going in Griffin's direction.

He looked up at me and gave a small smile. "I'll back your play, whatever you decide."

There were very few times when I allowed myself to have any doubts about Griffin's and my relationship. This was the reason for that. Everything in the way that he was holding himself told me that he absolutely hated the idea of me spending any time with Paul. However, like my grandmother, he was supporting my decision. Although, unlike my grandmother, I'm pretty sure he would have had a problem with me transporting Paul's body across state lines. I guess no relationship is perfect.

Chapter Sixteen

Walking into the diner the next morning with a reluctant Edwin, I was hoping I'd made the right decision. Paul had been eager for the meeting when I had contacted him the night before, but I wasn't really sure that he was approaching it with the same mindset that I was.

"There he is," Edwin tapped me on the shoulder and pointed to where Paul was sitting in the corner.

I nodded sharply and headed towards the small booth Paul had found. Paul smiled widely at me until he caught sight of Edwin who was following very closely behind.

"Who's he?"

"This is my friend, Edwin. Edwin is here as a…" I paused for a moment grasping desperately for a word that wouldn't make this awkward.

"Chaperone," Edwin interjected helpfully.

Nope, that wouldn't have been the word that I would have chosen.

"You're meeting me with a chaperone?"

I was right there with Paul at how ridiculous that sounded.

"He will be sitting right over there." I pointed out a table and was gratified when Edwin went and sat at it with a minimal amount of fuss. That was why he had been chosen for this role.

"At what point did you think you needed a chaperone to meet with me?" Paul asked as I took a seat opposite him.

"Since you decided to turn up out of the blue and disrupt my life."

"I'm not doing this to hurt you."

"Then why are you doing this?" I couldn't stop the exasperation in my voice.

"I'm doing it because I love you and I want to stop you from making the worst decision of your life."

I had to stop myself from rolling my eyes. "And why am I making the worst decision of my life?"

"Ever since you got involved with this guy you've become a magnet for trouble. I've heard the stories. You're finding dead bodies. You've been shot, you've been kidnapped. This guy is bad news."

It was interesting to see Paul's interpretation of the events of the past couple of years of my life. I never thought to place my bad luck when it came to finding bodies at Griffin's door. Clearly, Paul thought that I should. I wondered if he had shared this theory with my mother.

"None of that is Griffin's fault. My life in LA has just been a little more hectic than it should have been. That kind of thing happens all the time out here."

Luckily Paul couldn't see the face that Edwin pulled at that last statement. My friends had long ago come to the conclusion that this kind of thing could only happen to me.

"Paul, I need you to understand. I am happy here and I am in love with Griffin. There is nowhere that I would prefer to be than here."

"I don't believe you."

I gripped my hands tightly together to stop myself from braining my ex-fiancé with a napkin dispenser.

"Okay, Paul. I've tried to be as delicate about this as I can, but I need you to go home and leave me alone. I don't know what your plan was when you came here, but I am not running home with you. We are done, and have been for a very long time. Nothing is going to change that."

Once again I felt like I had put my point across with no room for misinterpretation.

"I don't think you mean that."

I had truly forgotten how stubborn Paul could be. I was just about to really let him have it when I felt myself getting hauled out of my seat. I looked up into Travis's smiling face as he tucked an arm around my waist.

"Hey, honey. Ready to get back to work?"

Paul stood up, a worried look on his face. It was interesting to note that Edwin just kept sipping his coffee, totally calm regarding the scene unfolding in front of him.

"Who is this guy?" Paul demanded.

I hesitated for a moment. I was once again grasping for an appropriate term but decided to go for simple, if only to prevent Travis from presenting his own interpretation.

"He's a friend."

I saw Travis's grin but I really did not want to take the time to describe the complexities of my relationship with Travis to Paul. For now 'friend' would have to do.

"So, you are the ex?"

Paul straightened under this new scrutiny. "You got a problem with that?"

Travis shrugged. "Don't really care. I just like to know where everybody stands. Word to the wise though. Her new man is not one you want to get in the way of. He knows people, unsavory people, if you get my drift."

I was reasonably sure that Travis was trying to be helpful. Then again, he could have been just messing with me because it amused him.

"I hope you heard what I said," I directed at Paul as I was being herded out of the diner by Travis. I glanced over at Edwin who raised a hand and waved at me as he pulled out his phone. It seemed my chaperone was fine with the way things had turned out.

"What are you doing here?" I demanded once we were outside.

"You don't have to thank me. The grateful expression on your face is enough."

I couldn't believe it. "This is not gratitude. I was trying to have an adult conversation with Paul to end this thing.

Now I'm going to have to do it all over again."

Travis gave me a wry smile. "Whatever you were doing, Trudie, it wasn't working. He was not going to listen to you. That man has one thing on his mind and it isn't going to be changed by a reasonable conversation over coffee."

I wondered if I was angry with Travis because I knew he was right. I had been able to see that Paul wasn't listening to me throughout the conversation. I had tried so hard to make him understand but it simply wasn't working.

"What did you mean by Griffin knowing 'unsavory people'?"

"He does know unsavory people. Usually he arrests them. But he knows them. Thought it might help the ex decide to leave town if he thought Griffin could do him some bodily damage."

"Oh yes, that was helpful."

Travis shrugged. "No harm in trying."

"How did you find me anyway?"

"Went by your place. Met your grandmother, by the way. Frightening woman. She must have been hell on wheels when she was younger."

I couldn't fault his perceptions.

"Griffin was there, looking miserable. I have to congratulate you. In all the years I have known the man, I have never managed to make him look quite so despondent. And, believe me, I have worked at it."

Trust Travis to make me feel worse than I already did. I quickly sent a text message to Griffin. I probably didn't need to. I was pretty sure that Edwin had filled him in on everything that had happened the second I had left the diner.

"So, where are we going?" I asked as I got in Travis's car.

"We're going back to the house. I think we need to have a better look around. It seems the attic got closed off around the same time that Moretti took up residence. There may be something else in there that is relevant to the case.

I knew it was slightly inappropriate, but I was pleased that we were going back to the job that I had wanted to do the entire time.

Chapter Seventeen

The greeting from Martha was as warm as ever, but I did manage to get a small smile from Eugene when we pulled up. I was going to put that in the win column.

"You've been making friends," Travis commented.

"I do try. Although this has proven to be a tougher sell than most."

"Why do you think that is?"

"This house seems to be out of step with the rest of the world. None of these people seem to have moved out of this place and lived their own lives. It's like they're trapped here, maybe as much as Johnny Moretti. I don't think that it is any surprise that the same staff that are living here now were all around when Johnny died."

Travis was watching me intently and I started to feel uncomfortable under his gaze. "What?"

His face broke with a smile. "No, you're right. I think that even though nobody is talking about it, what happened back then may have shaped the way this household is now."

The attic was exactly as I had left it two days earlier when I had found the mummified body.

"So, where did you want to start?" I asked.

Travis looked around at the multitude of boxes and chests. "Closest box. Keep an eye out for paperwork, journals, letters, anything that might look out of place. People have a tendency to hide things in books so go through those. Anything that looks interesting, put in a pile over there so we can go through it more closely."

I was more than a little surprised to find that combing through an attic of movie memorabilia with Travis Cooper was enjoyable. His knowledge of old movies and their stars showed a side of him that I had not expected to see.

"What are you smiling at?" he demanded as he was flicking the pages of an old pile of papers with an air of impatience.

"I never thought that this would be your thing," I said calmly. "I know it's my thing and I understand why I get excited over it. I just would have thought you were more of a modern action blockbuster person."

Travis shook his head. "I keep trying to make you understand that you are woefully underestimating me. I'm deeper than you think."

"I'm beginning to get that."

"Now that you know how deep and sensitive I am, are you going to leave Griffin and run away with me?"

"And you just had to ruin the moment, didn't you?"

Travis smiled. "I am very good at that, just ask any woman I go out with."

"So damaged," I said, shaking my head.

Travis laughed and went back to the papers in his hand.

"What are you looking at there?"

"It looks like a script for a movie. Doesn't have a name to it but it looks pretty interesting." He looked over at the magazine I had been reading for the past ten minutes. "What have you got?"

"A magazine article about Dorothy Stanhope and Martin Harrington."

"Anything interesting in there?"

I smiled grimly. "I'm going with the assumption that it is completely fiction."

"Usually a good assumption to make, especially at that time."

Travis got up and came to sit on the dusty ground next to me.

"Let's have a look at this."

As he read the article I looked over his shoulder at the accompanying photo spread. The article seemed to be a typical one from the 1950s. There were no salacious scandals and everything was managed within an inch of its life. The story was about Dorothy Stanhope and her life, including her amazing boyfriend Martin Harrington. It also talked about her loving relationship with her mother. I hadn't known much about Dorothy Stanhope's mother, but looking at the photos you could see that Virginia Stanhope had been a beautiful woman. While Dorothy and Martin lounged by the pool, her mother was in the background, dressed as if she was on her way to a fashion shoot. Dorothy was the focus of the article, but her mother seemed to be the one to draw the eye.

Travis sighed as he finished reading the article. "Just once, I would love to see a relationship that is exactly as advertised."

"What are you talking about?"

Travis eyed me patiently. "I'm saying that this article may be about the love between Martin and Dorothy, but the photos tell me he's sleeping with the mother."

"It's a sixty year old magazine. How on Earth can you make that kind of conclusion based on some old photos?"

"I'm a professional and believe me when I say that weird relationship couplings are my specialty." Travis blew out a breath. "He's hesitant with Dorothy in these photos. You can see he isn't sure how to approach her." Travis pointed to a photo of Martin with his arm slung casually around Dorothy's shoulders. "Here he's looking over Dorothy's head in the direction of the mother. That look on his face is knowing. He's been somewhere he knows he wasn't supposed to be. And he loves that he is getting away with it."

I did some calculations. I knew that Dorothy Stanhope's mother had been young when she was born, and the photos in the article showed a confident and beautiful woman in her prime. Despite the fact that Dorothy Stanhope had been a beautiful film star, there was no doubt that even at eighteen she was still very young. I could see why a young man would have gravitated towards the obviously sexually confident older woman. Still, he was supposed to be her daughter's boyfriend. That put it in the creepy file.

"Are you sure?"

"I'm as sure as I can be without actually seeing them do the deed."

This situation was just getting better and better. At least I knew that Dorothy wouldn't have cared one little bit based on what she'd told us about her feelings for Martin Harrington.

"How does that affect our search for a murderer?"

Travis shrugged. "If Harrington was sleeping with the mother, it indicates that there was no great love between him and Dorothy. That would usually drop him lower on the list of suspects."

"It might have been a blow to his pride that people thought he was being dumped by the most famous film star in the world for a mechanic," I ventured.

"Always a possibility." Travis put the magazine on the pile of possible leads. It was looking depressingly small considering the amount of time we had been going through the attic. "Have you found anything else that could be interesting?"

"There's a small box of fan letters."

"Only a small box?" Travis queried.

"That's what makes it interesting. If she kept all her fan mail, I would have expected this entire attic to be filled. But there is only this little box. That tells me that there must be something special about them."

Travis raised an eyebrow. "Nice deduction. Good to see my skills are rubbing off on you."

I loved how it all came back to him. I opened the box and passed some of the letters to Travis. "Here, Super Detective. See what you can do with these."

Travis grinned. As usual, sarcasm was completely lost on him.

I started reading my pile of fan letters and felt myself smiling. It really had been a nicer time back then. As part of my role as personal assistant to celebrities, I was regularly required to go through correspondence sent to my clients. Usually I found that a small percentage was nice, some were critical and some were immediately forwarded to police. There was nothing like celebrity to bring out the crazy in people. These letters were sweet and uplifting. There was the possibility that I was romanticizing that period in time. Chances were that I was only getting to see the best of what people had sent to Little Dottie. If this small box was a complete representation of the nice letters that people had sent, then it would show that people were no better back then than they were today. I wasn't sure why that was a depressing thought, just that it was.

"This is interesting." Travis waved a letter in my direction.

I went to grab it but he pulled back.

"What is it?"

"It seems to be a letter from Eugene."

"The gardener?" That was a little strange. "What does it say?"

"Well, it's a bit on the long side, but I'll give you the summary version. In this letter, Eugene waxes lyrical on Dorothy Stanhope's many virtues, including beauty, talent and general sweetness. He wrote at length on the subject." Travis flicked through the several pages of the letter. "Looks like Eugene had quite the crush on Dorothy Stanhope."

I nodded. "Like pretty much every other male on the planet at that time. It would have been more surprising if he didn't have a crush on her."

"Makes him a viable suspect," Travis commented.

"A gushing fan letter from sixty years ago makes him a viable suspect?"

"I'm not saying that he did it. I'm saying that there is a possibility that someone who took the time to write a virtual novel about her many attributes may have had a reason to get upset when some random guy turns up and sweeps her away from him. Especially if he was here all the time."

I could see his point. I didn't want to see his point, but I could see it, nonetheless. Despite the less than warm welcome I had received from Eugene, I had trouble believing that he could be a murderer. Of course, I only knew the elderly man who winced from the pain in his knees when he walked. I had no idea what he would have been like sixty years ago.

"Did you want to talk to him again?" I asked.

I could see Travis contemplating his next move. He shook his head. "No. The funeral is tomorrow. I'd like to see whether he goes and how he reacts to everything before questioning him again."

"So you'll be at the funeral?" I asked.

Travis nodded. "Always a good place to get information. Anyway, my understanding is that any funeral that has you in even a peripheral role is always going to be interesting."

"You've been talking to Tomas," I remarked wryly.

"He does look forward to you being involved when he's planning a funeral. It's almost indecent how much joy he gets out of it."

I had to agree with Travis there.

Chapter Eighteen

"You're in a lovely mood this morning, aren't you?" Tomas scrutinized my face and I could tell that he was not impressed with what he saw. I didn't blame him. I'd hardly slept the night before. My Grandma Rita and Miss Betsy had been in fine form coming up with plans to deal with the 'Paul situation'. Griffin had given up trying to talk them out of taking any action and had gone to bed early, claiming a headache for the first time in his life. The two elderly women had taken this as a sign that he would tacitly approve any crazy idea that they came up with. It had taken all my energy to disabuse them of that notion. I was still not entirely sure that they had accepted my edict that they leave the situation alone. I just hoped there wasn't going to be any collateral damage.

"I'm fine."

Tomas made a choking noise. "I really don't think that word means what you think it means."

I wiped my hand over my face. "You want to know the truth? My ex-fiancé turned up and is trying to break my engagement with Griffin. If that wasn't bad enough, my grandmother has arrived to 'take care of the situation' which is always a scary prospect, especially as she seems to have recruited some backup. And I am now working for Travis Cooper to try to work out who killed the sixty year old mummy in the attic of what was supposed to be the best job I had in my life. You're right. I'm not fine."

Tomas enveloped me in a hug. "I understand."

I was pretty sure that Tomas did not understand what I was going through, but I appreciated the sentiment. As he hugged me I looked over his shoulder and saw Helena, his cosmetician. I smiled broadly. I had worked with Helena before and marveled at her skills when it came to making the dead look amazing, especially the bodies that I brought her way. Helena huffed, spun around and stalked off.

I frowned as I pulled away from Tomas. "What's wrong with Helena?"

"She's been a bit petulant ever since I told her she wasn't to work on this body. Seems my description only made it seem like a challenge to her."

I should have realized. Helena had some quirks that it took some time to get used to. One of them was her seeming need to improve any corpse that came within her sphere of influence. It was no wonder she was mad at me.

"Don't worry," Tomas assured me. "She'll get over it. Just make sure that the next body you bring us is able to be worked on."

I grimaced at his nonchalant tone. "You say that as if I have a choice with these situations."

Tomas raised an eyebrow at me.

"Not funny," I grumbled. "Considering the mood I'm in, I would suggest you be a little more tactful."

"I could but I wouldn't enjoy these days quite so much if I did."

I grimaced at the comment. I could guarantee that I did not find these days enjoyable at all.

"Is that gorgeous detective of yours going to be joining us today?" Tomas asked as we walked over to the closed casket at the front of the room.

I shook my head. "No, he has another case. Something more recent."

Tomas nodded with an understanding look on his face. I still found it amazing. If Johnny Moretti had died in Dorothy Stanhope's attic in the last week, everyone would be all over the case. We wouldn't have been able to move for all the cops and media people. Instead we were able to find and bury the body with relative anonymity.

I looked down at the casket. There wasn't even a photo to signify the man who lay inside. It was all so impersonal, as if everyone felt that the sooner we got this over and done with, the happier everyone would be.

"Did you want to see the body?" Tomas queried.

I shivered. "Why would I possibly want to see his body again? I'm still having nightmares from the first time."

"People are weird. Maybe you need some closure," a new voice intruded.

"Not that kind of closure, Travis." I turned around to greet my work colleague. "You're early."

Travis shrugged. "I figured you'd be here and if anyone was feeling guilty they might come early, think they're alone and confess all to the dead body of their victim."

"Does that ever actually happen?" I asked skeptically.

"Not really, but I'm always hopeful."

I glanced around the room and smiled approvingly at Tomas.

"You've done a good job, are you sure you don't want to do my wedding?"

I laughed at the grimace on Tomas's face. It looked so out of place. I heard a noise at the doorway and I knew that I now sported an identical expression.

"What the hell?" I couldn't believe it. "Excuse me," I said tightly as I stalked off to greet the newest arrival to our little gathering.

I grabbed a smug looking Paul by the arm and pulled him into another room.

"Why are you here?" I demanded.

For one of the few times in his life, Paul looked completely stunned. "I wanted to talk to you."

"And you thought a funeral that I was attending for my job was the best place to do this."

"Of course not." Paul looked around, obviously a little surprised at where we had ended up. "I followed you from your home. I just wanted to speak to you without anyone around."

"Well, that's not going to happen." Even before I heard his voice I knew that Travis would not have allowed me to go anywhere out of his sight with Paul.

I didn't need to turn around to know that he was looming behind me, and I was pretty sure that Tomas was there as well. Of course, he was not so much there for protection, but more for the entertainment value.

"This state is pretty hard on stalkers and our prisons aren't exactly pleasant. I would suggest you want to turn around and go somewhere else. Anywhere else." I could see that Travis had reached the end of finding this situation amusing.

If we had been dealing with a normal person, that statement from Travis Cooper, at his most intimidating, would have been enough to make anyone reconsider their life choices. Paul was many things, but a coward was not one of them. This was going to require a different approach.

"Get out now."

Paul looked at me in surprise. I even think I'd managed to shock Travis. Tomas was just thoroughly entertained.

"I mean it. Get out now. I'm not interested in anything you have to say. I am dealing with a murder case right now. I don't have the time or inclination to deal with whatever garbage you are going through."

Paul opened his mouth as if to say something, but after peering at me carefully, he closed it and abruptly walked off.

"I love working with you."

"Thank you, Tomas." I barely managed to quell the irritation in my voice. Just once I would like a funeral that I was involved with to go off without a hitch or any drama. Maybe I was asking too much. If any event was going to bring high drama it would be a funeral or a wedding. Maybe I should elope.

"Nicely done," Travis commented.

I glanced back at the doorway to make sure that Paul had actually left and was not intending to make another appearance.

"Oh, for the love of…."

"What now?" Travis looked over to the doorway. "That can't be good."

Once again Travis showed his ability for understatement. The fact that Grandma Rita and Miss Betsy turned up so soon after Paul interrupted my day could only mean one thing.

"Please tell me that you're not following Paul."

The two women protested their innocence. It was interesting to see that Miss Betsy seemed to have the same lack of ability as I did when it came to lying. She looked guilty as hell and refused to look in my direction. No such problems for my grandmother. That woman was a professional.

"What are you doing here?"

"Now, Trudie. Don't get upset." I knew that voice of my grandmother's. It never boded well. "I just wanted to see what you did at this job you seem to love so much."

My grandfather had always said that she could make a politician blush with how well she could sell a blatant lie. Unfortunately for her, I was not in a buying mood. However, I was not in a place where I could argue the point about her true intentions for the day.

"This is not a social occasion. This is my place of work. You do not just drop in to see what I do. Anyway, today is not representative of what I spend the majority of my time doing."

I was going to ignore the inelegant snort that came from Tomas, as well as the raised eyebrow from Travis.

"You need to leave."

My grandmother looked shocked. Despite the animosity between her and my mother, my grandmother knew that I had been indoctrinated from birth to be painfully polite. Kicking my grandmother out of a funeral did not keep with my normal behavior. Luckily, Miss Betsy could see that I had reached the end of my patience, and ushered my protesting grandmother out of the building.

"You're going to pay for that," Travis murmured.

Once again the king of understatement made an appearance.

I glanced at my watch. "People should be arriving soon."

"That can't be good."

"What's wrong now?" I asked Travis, confused by the suddenly concerned expression on his face.

"This case just got a little more complicated," Travis murmured, his gaze focused on the group that had just walked into the funeral home.

We had no real suspects, no leads and, if I was being realistic, I doubted that this case could ever be solved. I failed to see how two elderly men accompanying Johnny Moretti's sister to the funeral was enough to make this situation more complicated.

"I think we need to call Griffin," Travis muttered.

That escalated way faster than I was expecting it to.

"For those of us in the group who are taking a bit more time to catch up, could you please explain what on Earth you are talking about."

"Those two men with Johnny Moretti's sister have spent the last several decades running a good proportion of illegal activities in certain areas of this city. If Johnny Moretti was in any way involved with them, the fact that he died a violent death just became much more understandable."

Tomas clapped his hands together. "I knew you wouldn't just bring me a dead body," he exclaimed.

He was right. I couldn't just bring him a simple dead body. Obviously my destiny was to always bring my funeral planner drama and excitement. Now that I thought about it, what sort of person had a funeral planner on speed dial?

Unfortunately Tomas's impression of a child on Christmas morning did not go unnoticed by our visitors and they were watching us curiously. I stepped forward and stopped when I felt Travis grab my elbow.

I looked up and was truly touched by the concerned expression he had on his face. "I'll be fine. They've come for a funeral. They don't really look like they are going to start a gang war here."

Travis reluctantly let me go and I walked over to the three elderly mourners. The two men stood on either side of Rosa Moretti, each of her hands were on their arms as if they were holding her up in her time of need. They themselves looked like they could be blown over by a strong wind. Despite Travis's warnings, I couldn't say that I felt frightened for my life facing these two aging gangsters.

"Miss Moretti, I'm so pleased you were able to make it here."

The older woman grasped my hand with a strength that surprised me. "I had to say goodbye. He was my brother." She hesitated for a moment. "Would it be possible for me to see him?"

I tried to choose my next words carefully. "I'm not sure if that is such a good idea."

"But I want to see him."

I could see the disappointment in Rosa's eyes and I glanced at her companions, hoping that they would realize how much of a bad idea Rosa seeing her brother would be.

One of the men who looked the least like the dangerous gangster that Travis had tried to convince me he was, patted Rosa on the arm. "It's been a long time, Rosa. That isn't Johnny anymore. It's better that you remember him like he was."

Rosa's eyes filled with tears. "I want to talk to him."

That we could kind of do. "If you'll follow me."

I led the small group to the next room where the service was to be held. The three of us stood back while Rosa slowly walked towards the coffin holding her brother.

The taller of the two men cleared his throat as we

watched the elderly woman start sobbing over the coffin holding her long-lost brother.

"You were the one who found him?"

After taking a moment to weigh up all my options when answering that question, I nodded.

He ran his hand through the very small amount of hair he still had on his head. "And you're the one organizing the funeral."

"Yes, I am."

I waited for the next question. The two men watched me keenly. "You know who we are?" the other man asked. He looked less like a gangster than the first man. More like the kindly old man who lived at the end of a suburban street. I was pleased that I had been called away from Travis before he had properly filled me in on the identity of these two men. Sometimes ignorance is your closest ally and I was more than happy to use it now.

"I'm assuming you're friends of Rosa's." I was hoping I was going to get left alone on this one.

"Johnny was a friend of ours back in the day. You could say he was a very close friend."

"I'm so sorry for your loss." Not the most original thing that I could have said, but in some circumstances I find it is better to fall back on standard social niceties.

I kept my eyes straight ahead as I watched Rosa, trying to look as innocent as possible. I could feel the two men staring at me intently as if trying to discern how I fit into this situation. I was relieved when I heard the sounds of new arrivals from the next room.

"I had better see who that is." I started moving away slowly, trying hard not to spook anyone. "When Rosa's finished please take a seat. The service will be starting very soon."

I started breathing normally again when I stepped through the doorway and saw that Dorothy Stanhope had arrived. She was accompanied by both Martha and Eugene. Eugene was watching her with a worried look on his face. After having seen the letter he had written to her so many years ago, I could see the devotion he had for her. Martha looked as if she would prefer to be anywhere else than here. I was not overly surprised to see that Martin Harrington was standing behind her, glaring straight at me as if this whole situation was somehow my fault.

I hurried forward and greeted the small group. As I reached them Dorothy grasped my hand.

"The service will be starting in a couple of minutes," I informed them. "Would you like to wait out here until then or would you prefer to go in?"

"We'll go in," Martha announced. It was interesting to see that she had taken the lead in this situation.

"Johnny's sister, Rosa, is currently in there with some friends saying her goodbyes."

A strange look that I couldn't interpret crossed Dorothy's face. "Maybe it would be better if we stayed out here. We'll let her have some time with him."

I could understand that. Despite the fact that Dorothy Stanhope was paying for Johnny to have a dignified send-off, we should probably not forget that his body had been found in her attic. At most funerals I had attended, that would make for an uncomfortable meeting with the family and friends of the deceased. I looked over and saw Tomas giving me the sign that the service was about to start.

I ushered the small group into the other room, my body tense at the possibility of a confrontation with Rosa Moretti. I needn't have worried. Rosa ignored the new arrivals. If it hadn't been for the stiff way she was holding herself, I could have made myself believe that she didn't care. I watched from the back of the room as the newest arrivals took their seats on the opposite side to Rosa and her friends. The two groups took great pains to ignore each other, making for what could only be described as an exceedingly awkward situation. I watched Martin Harrington as he walked to the front of the room. If I hadn't been looking directly at him, I wouldn't have noticed how he stiffened at the sight of the two elderly gentleman who had accompanied Rosa Moretti. I also would have missed the slow predatory smile that crossed the face of the man that Travis had explained to me was one of the more dangerous men roaming the streets of LA for the last several decades. It looked like they knew each other and my impression wasn't that they were old friends.

Chapter Nineteen

Just as the service began, the door I was standing next to opened slightly and Tomas indicated that my presence was required. I retreated from the room as discreetly as I could and turned to my friend.

"What's wrong? Do you need help with…..ouch, what was that for?"

I rubbed my arm where my supposed friend had just hit me, not hard but it was the surprise that hurt the most.

"That was Dorothy Stanhope," he hissed.

"Yes it was."

"You did not tell me that Dorothy Stanhope was involved."

"Considering your first reaction on finding out that she was attending was to assault me, are you surprised I didn't tell you? Anyway, she's not involved. Johnny Moretti was her old boyfriend from sixty years ago and his body was found in a trunk in her attic."

Tomas looked at me with a disbelieving expression. As I went over in my mind what I had just said, I figured that look was warranted. I probably deserved the slap as well. With a dramatic sniff in my direction Tomas spun around and stalked off.

"Wow, you're good with people."

"Could you please stop talking, Travis," I sighed.

"Whatever you want."

I could feel my forehead crinkling. That reasonable comment did not sound like it came from the Travis Cooper that I had grown to know and barely tolerate. I was missing something here.

I looked up and saw Griffin standing in the doorway.

"You just had to do it, didn't you?" I drawled.

Travis grinned. "I thought it was understood.

Dangerous people anywhere within your vicinity mean I have to call Griffin. It's a rule."

"Since when did you start following rules?"

"Since I discovered how much fun it is to watch you trying to dodge around that man's protectiveness."

"I hate working with you."

"And yet we seem to do it often. I don't think that's a coincidence."

He was right. "It isn't a coincidence. I just think the universe likes messing with me for entertainment purposes."

"I hear that you are in trouble again," Griffin said as he walked up to us.

"I'm not in trouble. Travis is being a mother hen. An extraordinarily annoying mother hen."

"Because that is how everybody describes Travis Cooper."

I really didn't like it when Griffin resorted to sarcasm.

"We have Bernie Deskin and Marky Russo in the next room," Travis interjected helpfully.

Griffin whistled beneath his breath.

"Martin Harrington is in there as well. He does not look happy," Travis added.

"Interesting."

"Why is that interesting?" I did not like the way the two men were acting as if everyone in the room knew what they were talking about. "I would have thought that wouldn't be a problem. Martin Harrington is a criminal defense lawyer. Why would it be a problem if he is in the same room as criminals? Isn't that a job requirement?"

Travis grinned. "Usually it is. Martin Harrington will accept money from anybody, and I do mean anybody. The man has the moral compass of a politician. But he has never acted as a lawyer for those two. Word is that they hate each other. Have done for years and nobody knows why."

I looked at the expressions on the faces of the two men

with me. "You don't think that it is a coincidence that they are together for this funeral, do you?"

Griffin shrugged. "It could be, but it's just a little strange. Those three men have skillfully avoided being in the same place for decades and now they are coming together. Seems like an unlikely set of circumstances."

"So you're going to be looking into Johnny Moretti's death now?"

Griffin shook his head regretfully. "Three men who hate each other being in the same room for the first time in decades does not constitute a serious lead."

"Really?"

"Look, if you guys come up with something concrete, I will present it to the Lieutenant and push for us to investigate. Do you have anything?"

I looked at Travis and my shoulders slumped. "No." We had ideas but nothing that would constitute proof.

"Then my hands are tied."

I could tell that Griffin was as frustrated as I was. He may have been trying to rationalize the fact that this murder was so old that the department couldn't justify the expense or manpower it would take to follow it up, but I could see that not even trying went against everything he stood for.

I heard Tomas clear his throat behind us. "The service is finished. Everyone is moving into the other room for refreshments."

Travis arched an eyebrow in Griffin's direction. "Want to join us? This could be interesting."

I did not like the way Travis said that. I also really didn't like the answering grin that was crossing Griffin's face.

The room Tomas had set aside for the refreshments had light streaming in through large windows. Even though it was quite small, the two groups managed to still keep a sizable distance between them. Despite the fact that I was employed by Dorothy Stanhope I still felt drawn to

Rosa Moretti.

"Wait here a moment," I murmured to my two companions who I knew would pitch a fit if they knew my intentions.

I couldn't help but feel a little trepidation as I walked up to Rosa Moretti. Travis's warning about the two men who accompanied her kept spinning in my head.

"I hope you were happy with the service."

Rosa looked up at me and smiled despite the tears I could see in her eyes. "Thank you. At least I know he is at rest now."

"He won't be at rest until we find out who did this to him." The larger of the two men accompanying Rosa had decided to make his presence felt.

I felt a slight shiver of fear creep up my spine at that voice. It wasn't what was said but you could imagine this man tormenting puppies for fun.

"These are friends of Johnny's. They insisted on bringing me here today." Rosa smiled gratefully.

"I'm Bernie Deskin and this here is Marky Russo but I'm pretty sure your watchdogs have already told you who we are." The smaller of the two men put his hand forward and grasped mine firmly. I resisted the temptation to look over and see how my two protectors were dealing with the familiarity Bernie was showing me.

"I hear you've been asking questions about what happened to Johnny." The grip on my hand tightened, not yet to the point of pain but the message was clear.

Bernie let go of my hand and smiled. "Good afternoon, Detective."

Even without Bernie's sarcastic greeting I could feel the heat at my back as a large over-protective cop decided to make his presence felt. Obviously this conversation had gone on for too long.

"We were just thanking your fiancée for her diligent work in making sure that Johnny could rest in peace."

I did not like the fact that somehow this man knew

about my personal life with Griffin.

"I'm sorry for your loss," I murmured to Rosa as I was swiftly ushered away.

Travis was shaking his head as I walked back to him.

"You were the kind of kid who always jumped before thinking, weren't you?"

"She's Johnny's sister. What was I supposed to do, ignore her?"

From the looks on the two men's faces I could see that was their preferred option.

"I wonder what he's doing here."

I followed Travis's eyes to the doorway where Avery Harrington was standing.

"I'm assuming to meet his brother," I ventured.

"Maybe."

Avery walked over to his brother and whispered in his ear. Martin looked down at him with an irritated expression. Avery ducked his head and left the room quickly.

"What was that about?" I murmured.

Griffin shrugged. "Those two have always had a strange relationship. Avery is quite a bit younger than Martin, and he has always been treated like he shouldn't be a part of the family firm."

"It looks like he is planning on leaving," I commented. "Did you want to talk to him before he goes?"

Travis shook his head. "I don't think the questions we have to ask would really be appropriate considering the setting."

We watched as Martin said his goodbyes. I saw Eugene stiffen as Martin ducked his head and kissed Dorothy on the cheek, the animosity obvious for everyone to see.

Martin straightened and headed straight for us.

"There will be no questions asked of Miss Stanhope unless I am in attendance."

I could see why this man had such a sterling reputation amongst police officers.

Griffin stiffened beside me and I could see him nod at the demand. He was a police officer, bound by the rules of law.

Unfortunately for Martin Harrington, Travis Cooper was not a police officer and therefore was not bound by the whole lawyer being present rule. I could see from the grin on his face that he knew it.

"I've just got a few questions, nothing you need to be worried about." Travis was truly gifted in the way he could say those words, but everyone in the room knew that he meant the complete opposite to what he was saying.

Martin's face flushed an ugly shade of red. "I keep telling Dorothy that paying you to look into this is the biggest waste of money. Your specialty is cheating spouses and deadbeats."

The smile on Travis's face did not slip one bit. He did not seem to be at all perturbed by the attack. "That is true."

Harrington looked triumphant and started to walk away.

"So," Travis drawled casually. "In keeping with my skill set, I was wondering how long you were sleeping with Dorothy Stanhope's mother?"

The room went silent. Expressions ranged from shock to a morbid curiosity to hear the answer. The most telling expression was on Martha's face. It was completely unsurprised. In that moment her eyes met mine and I was shocked by the anger in them.

Martin Harrington turned around slowly. "What did you say?"

"We have reason to believe that while you were Dorothy Stanhope's boyfriend, you were also sleeping with her mother."

So much for being discreet at a funeral. I sneaked a glance at Tomas and could see his eyes sparking with excitement. It looked like once again I had delivered on an entertaining funeral. I really should stop doing that.

I held my breath as Harrington stalked back towards us. "Keep out of my business or I will make you regret the day you met me," he hissed before walking away while refusing to look at anyone else.

"Too late," muttered Travis.

"I thought you weren't going to say anything."

Travis shrugged his shoulders, a wry grin making its way across his face. "I know, but the timing was perfect and there was no way that he was expecting us to have that kind of information. At least we know that he was having an affair."

"He didn't confirm anything," I protested.

"Course he did. He reacted exactly like most men do when they are caught with their pants down. Badly and with threats."

"Great, I can't see how that helps us at all."

"I just want to put it out there that I like him for the murder," Travis said, decisively.

'Any reason for that, other than your obvious dislike of the man?"

"No," said Travis. "I just really like him for the murder."

Out of the corner of my eye I could see Griffin shaking his head. I don't know what he was worried about. He could walk away from this mess. I was the one stuck in the middle of it. I kept an apologetic smile on my face as I walked up to Dorothy, Eugene and Martha. "I'm terribly sorry about that." I waved my hand in Travis's direction.

"I always wondered," Dorothy murmured. I couldn't tell if she was angry or relieved at the revelation.

From the waves of anger that were coming from Martha, I could tell she was furious.

As Eugene ushered Dorothy away, she stopped and put a hand on my arm. "I need to know what happened."

I looked in her eyes and I think I was beginning to understand. Dorothy Stanhope had been trapped in whatever happened sixty years ago. Johnny's funeral was her first step out of that mess.

I watched Dorothy and Eugene walking away and I could see the difference already. He stood straighter as though he was relishing the chance to show her she could depend on him. As he spoke to her I saw a slight smile cross her face. Sighing heavily I turned, only to be stopped by Martha. I caught my breath as I looked down at her. In my lifetime I had dealt with some extraordinarily objectionable human beings. I had been shot, kidnapped and assaulted, but I had never had a look of such pure loathing directed at me. Not for the first time I wondered what I had done to earn this woman's enmity.

"You need to drop this now," she hissed. "Nothing is going to bring him back and you are just causing her pain by chasing ghosts."

Martha let go of my arm and I had to resist the urge to rub where she had gripped me. As she walked away I noticed that she deliberately avoided looking at Rosa Moretti and her friends. The same couldn't be said for Bernie Deskin. He was watching Martha very carefully.

As I walked back to Griffin and Travis I was intercepted by Rosa. "Thank you again."

I smiled briefly and as they turned away I felt Bernie bump against me. As I went to steady him I felt a piece of paper being shoved into my hand.

"I want to talk to you without the cop," he hissed. "Meet me when you're finished here."

"You okay?" Griffin asked.

I curled my hand around the piece of paper. "Sure."

He dragged his hand through his hair. "Look, I have to get back to work."

"Sure." I really wanted to say something more substantial, but obviously that was beyond me. I knew if I said something else then that would constitute lying. If anyone knew how bad a liar I was, it was the man standing in front of me.

As it was, his eyes narrowed. "Is there anything I need

to know about?"

A direct question. I was in trouble.

"Trudie, I need to talk to you."

I could have kissed Tomas.

"I need you to sign some of these forms."

Heroes come in all shapes and sizes. For me it was a man who was pedantic about paperwork.

"I'll see you tonight." I waved Griffin away as I concentrated really hard on getting my signature just right.

"He's gone," Tomas commented wryly.

"What do you mean?"

From the look on Tomas's face I could tell that my attempt at innocence was a complete waste of time.

"Sure, we'll play it that way," he mumbled as he grabbed the papers and stalked away.

"Now you've done it," Travis commented.

Yes, I had. I was going to have to send him a gift basket, or organize another funeral. I was pretty sure I knew which of those options he'd appreciate more.

I unfolded the piece of paper that Bernie had given me. On it was written an address.

"Okay, partner, we've got someplace to be."

"The fact you waited until Griffin was out of the door to tell me that means that I'm not going to like what happens next, doesn't it?"

I grimaced. "I doubt it."

"Where are we going?"

"Bernie Deskin wants to talk to us."

"Do you need me to tell you how bad an idea that is?"

I understood why Travis was so reluctant. He knew far more about Bernie Deskin than I did. I was assuming that very little of that knowledge was positive.

"Right now, do we have anything that looks like a lead?"

Travis blew out a breath. "No."

"Is there a possibility that this man can at least give us some information that could help us?"

"He would be our best chance."

I could tell that it pained Travis to admit that.

"That means we need to meet him."

Travis's shoulders slumped and I could see he agreed. Albeit very reluctantly. "We are never going to tell Griffin about this."

Like that was going to stop him finding out.

Chapter Twenty

When Bernie had shoved that address into my hand, I had expected it to lead to a dingy bar in a back alley, filled with men who wouldn't think twice about dumping my body in the ocean. What we found was a large corporate office. It was one of those offices where you walk up to the front desk and half expect the person there to call security and have you tossed out. The woman looked like she was going to do exactly that right up until the point Travis smiled at her. It was smooth sailing from that moment on. She immediately got in touch with Bernie Deskin's office and we were ushered up to the top floor with views across the city. Whoever said crime didn't pay had never walked into this office.

"He'll be with you in a moment."

Travis and I were left alone in the office looking out at the city through full length windows.

"This is a bad idea. You know he'll find out, don't you? And when he does, I'm going to be the one he blames."

If only that were true I wouldn't be so worried. Griffin was perfectly capable of placing the blame exactly where it belonged. On me. Travis would just be collateral damage. I probably should have more concern for the predicament I had put him in.

"We need to know what happened," I hissed. "This is our best chance. He won't do anything here. We're perfectly safe." I really hoped that was true.

"Miss Eyre, Mr Cooper, so pleased you could make it."

Bernie Deskin came into the office and sat behind the desk, a large smile on his face. It did not make me feel any better.

I willed my hands to stop shaking. "You wanted to speak to us without a police presence."

Bernie looked at me keenly. "I had been hoping you would understand that I wanted to see you alone."

Travis pitched his voice low. "That was never going to happen. Your choice was me or Detective Griffin. Those were the only options available to you."

Bernie's eyes sparkled. "I'm beginning to see that."

There was silence for a moment as Bernie watched us as if deciding what to tell us. "How much do you know?"

Travis shook his head. "That's not how this works. You tell us what we want to know and then we might be more amenable to sharing what we have."

I was impressed. My understanding was that what we knew amounted to a big pile of nothing. Anything Bernie had to tell us would be far more valuable than what we already had. It looked like Travis was going to try to bluff Bernie Deskin. And he thought I was the reckless one.

Bernie frowned. I could see he didn't like this situation at all but we were holding firm.

I could see the moment that he decided to let us win this round.

"Marky and I grew up with Johnny. The three of us together could tackle anything. We never had any secrets between us. We were closer than brothers."

His eyes glazed as he seemed to become lost in memories.

"Johnny started working in a garage. He didn't want to get involved in the kind of things Marky and I got involved with. He wanted to make an honest living for himself and to help his mother out. He always said he couldn't take care of his mother from inside a jail cell."

So far Johnny sounded like a good guy.

"What happened?" I asked. "We know that Johnny met Dorothy Stanhope at the garage."

Bernie shook his head. "You need to go back before that time. Johnny meeting the great Dorothy Stanhope wasn't the moment when everything started to go wrong for him. Three months before that Johnny met another girl and he just lost his mind over her. We all told him that she was going to drag him down. We could all see it but he couldn't. He was completely in love and just lost the ability to see anything other than this woman."

"And that woman was…?"

"Martha Robbins."

It took me a moment to catch up with the rest of the group. "Martha, as in housekeeper to Dorothy Stanhope, Martha."

Bernie nodded. "Course she wasn't working at the house then. She'd left school and was working elsewhere. She met Johnny at the movies one day and he just fell for her completely. She was a wild one back then. Would give anything a try once."

I looked over at Travis. I wondered if he was having as much trouble as I was believing that the Martha who hated me for disrupting her life was the same wild Martha that Bernie was talking about.

"So what happened? Did he fall for Dorothy and dump Martha?" I could understand that and I could understand if she had some bitterness. At that time Dorothy Stanhope was the biggest star in the world. Martha never stood a chance. The second Dorothy crooked her finger, Johnny would have come running.

Bernie shook his head. "Johnny got involved with Dorothy Stanhope because Martha Robbins wanted to hurt her. She wanted Dorothy to fall for Johnny and then get her heart ripped out when Johnny chose Martha over her."

I could feel myself frowning at Bernie's revelation. "So Martha set up her boyfriend with Dorothy Stanhope, and believed that when she fluttered her eyelashes he would come running right back to her. That he would willingly leave one of the most famous and beautiful women of their generation." I was having some trouble with that scenario.

"Why not, she'd already managed to seduce Martin

Harrington away from Dorothy Stanhope. And her mother if what you said at the funeral was correct." Bernie shook his head. "I was surprised to hear about the mother, but considering the kind of man he is, maybe I shouldn't be."

It was interesting to hear the alleged criminal kingpin making moral judgments. Out of the corner of my eye I could see that Travis had straightened at the mention of an affair with Martha. So much for his much vaunted radar when it came to weird relationships. We had totally missed that one. I was almost feeling bad about the amount of information Bernie was providing us with when compared to the pathetic amount we had been able to uncover.

"Why are you telling us this?" I couldn't help feeling that I was missing an ulterior motive.

"I want Martin Harrington to go to prison for Johnny's murder."

That was pretty definite. "Why do you think Martin Harrington killed Johnny?" I was curious to see whether there was a reason or whether Bernie was joining Travis in really just wanting to put Martin Harrington in jail. So far all we had was a romantic triangle or quadrangle or something else that was really disturbing if you thought about it too hard. I was really trying not to think too much about it.

"Harrington may have been playing around with Dorothy and her mother but he fell hard for Martha."

I looked over at Travis and could see his raised eyebrow. I was having trouble with this too. I couldn't quite reconcile the dour woman who obviously hated the very sight of me for ruining her peaceful life with the seductive femme fatale who was able to twist men around her finger with no effort whatsoever.

Bernie stood up from his desk and stood in front of the window, looking out at the view.

"Harrington made the mistake of coming into our part of the city looking for Johnny. Johnny was not a big guy. He was good-looking but he was pretty small, especially compared to Harrington."

Bernie curled his hands into fists and I could imagine him as a young man, confident and a force to be reckoned with. I had the feeling Martin Harrington had learned that fact first-hand.

"Marky and I came across that piece of garbage beating up on Johnny. He was going to kill him."

"What happened next?"

Bernie turned around and smiled. It was not a nice smile. "We showed him the error of his ways. Wanted to make sure that he never touched Johnny again."

Considering the hatred that I had seen in Martin Harrington's eyes at the funeral I would guess that the message had been received, loud and clear.

"He didn't turn you in?" I queried.

Once again I got that smile from Bernie that I knew was going to haunt me in my sleep. "He had more secrets to hide than we did. No way was he going to risk them coming out."

"What kind of secrets?"

"We knew he was cheating on Dorothy Stanhope with Martha."

I nodded.

"We now know that he had been having an affair with Dorothy Stanhope's mother. He couldn't be sure we didn't know about that back then."

I nodded again.

"And for the past sixty years Martin Harrington has been embezzling from Dorothy Stanhope."

My mouth dropped open.

"Really," drawled Travis.

I had to agree with his skepticism. "That seems to be an awfully long time to commit a crime." It also seemed to be a long time for this man to keep quiet about it. Considering the animosity I had already seen between these men, I would have thought this information would have seen the light of day way before now.

Bernie chuckled. "He set it up back when she was raking in the dough. He was smart and only took a little bit in relation to what she was earning. Now that she doesn't earn anything it is harder for him to hide what he's done. But if he puts a stop to the embezzlement, people will notice the change. He's stuck."

"Is there any way to prove what he has been doing?" I asked.

Bernie pulled a file from his desk and passed it to me.

"There should be enough information here to get you started."

I opened the file and found bank records, invoices and receipts.

"How did you get this information?"

"In my line of business I generally find it useful to get information on people that I meet who interest me. It can help with difficulties down the line."

As I flicked through the pages I found some of the records were decades old. "How long have you been keeping this information?"

"When Johnny started seeing Dorothy Stanhope he came to me with his suspicions that Harrington might be skimming a bit off the top. He asked me to look into it. I found some information and then he disappeared. After that there didn't seem to be any use."

"But you still kept collecting the information."

Bernie gave me that smile of his again. "Let's just say that it became something of a hobby."

I still had trouble understanding. "Why didn't you tell somebody about this sooner, like last century sooner?"

Bernie shrugged. "I guess I was waiting for the right time. This seems to be the right time."

I could feel a line of sweat making its way down my back. Despite his advanced years this was a man that you did not want to turn into an enemy.

"Did you know that she loved him?"

Bernie raised an eyebrow. I knew it wasn't really the

kind of information that he was expecting, but for some reason I wanted him to know. "Dorothy Stanhope. She really loved him. She believed in him"

Bernie sighed regretfully. "That is unfortunate. I can guarantee that he might have ended up being fond of her, but he was obsessed with Martha Robbins. The fact he seduced another woman because she wanted to hurt her was proof of that. That woman turned Johnny into something he wasn't. A part of me is glad that he died because I don't think he could have lived with the man she turned him into."

I knew it wasn't a popular opinion in this room, but I was going to voice it anyway. "Is there any chance that Martin Harrington isn't the killer?"

From the looks on Travis's and Bernie's faces I could tell that wasn't the preferred outcome.

"We don't always get what we wish for. It just seems too easy to assume that Harrington is the killer and disregard everything else purely on the fact that he is a lousy human being."

"I won't allow Johnny's death to go unanswered." Bernie's voice was pitched low and the threat was obvious. "Someone is going to pay for it."

Travis cleared his throat. "How long do we have?"

"Forty-eight hours."

Chapter Twenty-One

Travis and I were silent as we walked to the car.

"Are we going to tell Griffin?"

Travis looked at me as if I was crazy. "You want to tell the police that we have forty-eight hours to find the killer of a man who died over sixty years ago or one of the city's leading citizens is going to face a truly gruesome death?"

I really didn't want to.

"Okay, I'm starting to get confused. Who was Johnny Moretti? Was he the sweet guy who was the love of Dorothy's life, was he the bad boy doing whatever he needed to do to get ahead, or was he Martha's puppet in some twisted revenge plot?"

Travis shrugged. "He could have been either or he could have been all of those things. People are complicated."

"At least now we know what Martha was lying about."

Travis swung open the door to the car. "I think it is time that we had another little discussion with Martha."

"You expecting anything other than more lies?" I asked as I got in the car.

"No, but sometimes the lies can be just as telling as the truth."

Sitting across from Martha I still had trouble with the description of her as some kind of femme fatale.

"What exactly are you accusing me of?"

I could see that Travis was trying to be diplomatic. I could also see that he was completely out of his depth. His charm might work on most women but Martha was looking at him like something she had scraped off the bottom of her shoe.

"During the course of our investigation we have uncovered some information which leads us to believe that you were in a relationship with Johnny Moretti."

I could see the relief in Travis's eyes when I jumped in. I figured that Martha couldn't stand the sight of me anyway. It wasn't like I could make the situation worse.

"Of all the contemptible…"

I waved my hand. "It's no use denying it. According to Johnny's friends he was obsessed with you, even willing to seduce another woman for you."

"That's ridiculous."

I looked over at Travis, wondering if he had also seen the flash of triumph in Martha's eyes. She might have been denying the accusation, but there was no hiding that even after six decades she was still proud of what she had done. A part of me felt slightly ill at that thought. I could not understand why someone would hold onto a grudge for that long.

I gentled my voice. "What did Dorothy do to you? Why did you hate her so much?"

I could feel Martha's eyes on me. "You have no idea what you are talking about."

"Martha." The three of us turned. Dorothy was standing in the doorway, Eugene hovering behind her. Dorothy's eyes narrowed as she took in the scene before her. "What is going on?"

I swallowed the lump in my throat. I really had not wanted Dorothy to find out any of this until I had put it all together, written down several draft copies, and practiced in front of a mirror so I could deliver this blow in the most gentle way possible. Eugene's eyes were begging me not to hurt her in any way. I really wish I didn't have to.

"We have reason to believe that Martha knew Johnny Moretti very well and may have instigated his relationship with you to hurt you." Travis had obviously decided that the blunt approach was the way to go.

Dorothy gave out a short bark of laughter. "Don't be ridiculous. I've known Martha since I was a child. She is not capable of doing anything like that."

A flash of anger crossed Martha's face. I looked over at Travis. I think Dorothy had just accomplished in one sentence what hours of us asking questions was not going to achieve.

"What would you know about what I'm capable of? I spent my life being a toy for you."

Dorothy looked shocked at the sudden attack by Martha.

"I was expected to be your perfect friend. My mother was paid extra for me to play with you. I was always told that if you were happy then we would get more money. It didn't matter that I wanted to do something else. I was no better than a doll that you could play with or toss aside at any time."

I winced at the description. That sounded like a pretty miserable way for a child to grow up. No wonder Martha looked angry all the time. She looked over at me and her eyes narrowed.

"You walk in here so excited to have this job." It looked like Martha had decided that I was in some way to blame. "You watch her movies and you think you know the great Dorothy Stanhope. You don't know the spoiled little girl. She was always so perfect and I was never even close. When I was bad my mother wanted to know why I couldn't be more like her and when I was good, she was always better."

For the first time I saw some real emotion in Martha's eyes. There was some serious anger going on there.

Dorothy put her hand on Martha's shoulder. "I'm so sorry. I didn't know."

Martha shook the hand off. "Don't give me your false sympathy. You couldn't care less. You got everything you wanted. People fawned over you and I got shoved to the side, every time. Even by my own mother."

"I never asked for that."

"Is that why you got your boyfriend to seduce Dorothy."

I should have known that Travis would be the one to make a bad situation so much worse.

Dorothy's eye's widened. "What?"

Genuinely frightened of how Travis would explain this situation to an emotionally delicate Dorothy, I decided to step in to try to make this easier.

"We have discovered that Martha was Johnny Moretti's girlfriend. We believe she was the one who set up the meeting with him and encouraged him to be friendly to you."

Dorothy's hand flew to her mouth. "Why would you do that?"

The expression that crossed Martha's face was ugly. "Because you got everything you wanted and I got nothing. I wanted you to know how it felt to lose out to me."

"Wasn't it enough that you had taken Martin Harrington from her?"

Dorothy gasped. I could see Eugene step up behind her and put an arm around her shoulder. I couldn't help but hope that he had never been involved with Martha. I didn't think any of us could handle that.

Martha smiled nastily. "That really didn't take much of an effort. I think the mother was more upset about that considering she had been sleeping with him for so long. Why do you think she kicked me out of the house?"

"Did you know he was embezzling from Dorothy?"

Martha shrugged calmly. "Doesn't surprise me."

As I watched Dorothy Stanhope, I wanted to tell Travis to stop. I'd always believed that it was better to know the truth, but at this moment I was questioning the wisdom of that belief. Dorothy looked so pale and fragile. Eugene's face was blazing in anger, desperate to find a way to fix this for Dorothy. Martha looked serene and I knew that she would never show remorse for what she had done. She was getting her revenge on Dorothy Stanhope. It might have been sixty years too late, but she was enjoying it. I felt sick that we were playing a part in this disaster.

"Did you care about Johnny Moretti at all?" I asked softly.

Martha lifted one shoulder. "He did what I wanted him to do." She looked over at Dorothy triumphantly, but I saw a flicker of something in her eyes.

"He started having second thoughts, didn't he?" Martha stared at me with a stony look on her face and I knew I had her. "That letter that he sent Dorothy. If he was part of your plan to destroy her, that letter would have been far more destructive and mean." I couldn't help but smile. "Everyone has been telling us that Johnny Moretti was a good guy who got caught up in something. He loved you and would do anything for you, but even he couldn't be as cruel as you wanted him to be."

Martha pursed her lips together. "You're a child. You don't know anything."

"Johnny knew that you were dragging him down, didn't he? Did he want to leave you as well?"

Martha shook her head. "No, he still adored me. I knew he was breaking but I just needed him to finish. He couldn't even do that properly."

"Did you kill him?" Travis's question dropped in the middle of the room and I could see his hand drop behind his back where I knew that a gun was holstered. We all took in a breath as we waited for the answer.

Martha smiled in a way that was truly ugly. "I didn't need to kill him to destroy him. I just needed to walk away. He would never recover from that."

Now I really felt sick.

"Get out of my house." Dorothy's voice rang through the room. A part of me was surprised that she was finally stepping forward and taking control of the situation.

Martha stood up with a smirk on her face and silently left the room.

"Aren't you going to arrest her?" Eugene glared at Travis.

Travis sighed. "I'm not the police. I don't have the power to arrest her even if we had any actionable evidence at all. Which we don't."

Eugene looked stunned by that statement.

"Nothing that she admitted to could constitute a crime," I said gently.

"So she gets away with what she did."

I didn't blame Eugene for the anger he was feeling. I could see it reflected in the faces of everyone in the room.

"Unfortunately, being a lousy human being is not a criminal offense."

Dorothy sat down heavily on the couch. "How could I not have known?"

"I don't think anyone would have been able to see that coming. You knew her from when you were a child. It's only natural that you trusted her."

"And Martin's been stealing from me."

I wished that I could wipe away the sadness in her eyes.

"We've come across some evidence which seems to indicate that he has been embezzling money from you for a very long time."

Travis cleared his throat. "I think our next stop should be the police. From what we can see he's been stealing from you for decades. This is going to be a big case and we need expert fraud investigators."

"You're right." Dorothy seemed to be pulling herself together. "It needs to be done." She looked over at Travis with a pleading look on her face. "Can you do it? I can't bear to sit there with people who think I'm an idiot for letting myself get taken advantage of in this way."

I grasped her hand. "You're not an idiot for trusting these people," I said fiercely. "They betrayed you. All the wrong done here is on them, not on you."

Dorothy gave me a slight smile. "You're very sweet but I should have been paying better attention. If I hadn't been so wrapped up in myself I would have realized what was right in front of me. Maybe now I can do better."

Chapter Twenty-Two

I sat quietly in the car as Travis guided it through the city.

I looked up when Travis cleared his throat.

"What's wrong?"

"Something is going on inside that head of yours and I'm just a little concerned where it is going to lead us.

"Did it seem strange to you that Martha was not bothered at all that she was ordered out of the only home she's known for most of her life?"

Travis nodded. "She would have to be in her late seventies or early eighties. She's not going to find another job, and I think her days of bending men to her will might be behind her."

"I wouldn't be so sure of that."

Travis grunted in reply. I noticed his eyes kept flicking up to the rear view mirror.

"What's going on?"

"We're being followed."

"What?" I twisted around in my seat.

"Somebody has been following us really badly for most of the day."

"What do you mean?"

"I mean that someone with zero skills has been following us all day. I'm pretty sure it's your ex-fiancé."

I dropped my head. "Please tell me that you're kidding me."

"I'm afraid not but that isn't what's worrying me. We've picked up another car following us and I think they do know what they're doing."

"What do you mean by that?"

"I mean that whoever it is, they were following at a

distance and now they're speeding up. They don't care that we know they are there. Have you got your seatbelt on?"

"Of course I have."

"Whatever happens, don't tense up."

Before I could reply to that ridiculous piece of advice the car lurched forward.

"Did they just...?"

Travis gripped the wheel even harder if that was possible. "They're trying to push us off the road."

I grabbed my phone but dropped it when we lurched forward again. Out of the corner of my eye I saw a black SUV with tinted windows coming up beside us.

"Hold on," yelled Travis as the SUV swerved into us and forced us to the side of the road. As we were pushed towards the lone tree on the embankment I closed my eyes, waiting for the inevitable pain that was to come. I found in that moment my only thought was Griffin and how I really wanted to feel his strong arms around me one more time.

The impact, when it came, was shocking, more so because I didn't feel anywhere near as much pain as I had been expecting. In the last desperate seconds Travis had managed to maneuver the car to minimize the damage to the two of us.

"Are you okay?" I looked over to see Travis frantically trying to get hold of his gun as the SUV pulled up next to us.

"Yeah, you?"

"Good. I want you to stay down. Can you get hold of your phone?"

I looked around. That phone that had flown out of my hands was now nowhere to be seen. "No."

Travis finally managed to pull out his gun just as the SUV drove off.

"What the...?"

A smaller car pulled up and a figure got out and raced towards us. He pulled open the door on my side.

"Trudie, are you okay?"

I was shocked that Paul was the one rescuing me.

"What are you doing here?" I asked as Paul helped pull me out of the car.

"I've been following you."

I turned to help Travis crawl over to my side of the car and get out. I couldn't handle the thought that Paul had been following me all day. I was working on dealing with my life one step at a time. First step was getting the man with the gun out in the open where he was at his most effective. Once we had disentangled Travis from the front car seat I turned around to find that Grandma Rita and Miss Betsy had arrived on the scene. I wish I was less surprised by the fact that Miss Betsy had a gun pointed directly at Paul.

Paul was holding his hands as high in the air as they could possibly go. "Trudie, why on Earth does that woman have a gun pointed at me?"

Despite hearing the fear in his voice I didn't have the energy to gently introduce him to the Second Amendment.

"Don't worry, you'll get used to it."

Grandma Rita gave a little sob and ran into my arms, squeezing tightly. Despite the fact that I felt far better than I expected after being in a car that had hit a tree, it still wasn't the best course of action she could have taken.

"What are you doing here?"

Miss Betsy answered as Grandma Rita seemed incapable of speech.

'We've been following him." She gestured towards Paul with her gun and I could see the fear on his face increase.

I managed to set Grandma Rita away from me. "You're telling me that Paul has been following me and you have been following him. All day."

Grandma Rita nodded.

Travis pointed a finger at Paul. "I spotted you miles back." He then pointed at Grandma Rita and Miss Betsy. "I didn't see you though."

Miss Betsy drew herself up and gave Travis her most haughty look. "Of course you didn't. I was tailing him, not you."

"I didn't see you either," Paul interrupted.

Grandma Rita rolled her eyes. "Of course you didn't. This woman is a professional."

Before I came to Hollywood I had truly not understood the wide range of skills that an ex-stuntwoman was expected to have. Miss Betsy had introduced me to firearms training, breaking and entering, and now it seemed that trailing a suspect was another skill she was hiding in her vast repertoire. If there was a zombie apocalypse I knew who I wanted by my side.

Once Grandma Rita had determined that I was in no danger, she pulled Paul aside and started explaining to him why stalking her granddaughter was a very bad idea. Miss Betsy stood in the background, glowering, making sure she kept that gun of hers in view. Travis and I sat on the edge of the road, both of us dealing with what had happened in our own way.

I looked over at the twisted wreckage of the car. "We can keep this from Griffin, right?"

"Sure," Travis said with far more sarcasm than I needed right now. "No way he's going to find out about this."

We sat there quietly contemplating the hunk of metal against the tree.

"I know I have never said this before but I want you to know that you are amazing."

Travis raised an eyebrow at me. "You have concussion, don't you?"

I shook my head and the fact it didn't hurt me almost made me weep with joy.

"I'm giving credit where credit is due. We were just run off the road. We should have been killed or, at the very least, injured really badly, but I feel fine. In fact, I feel pretty damn good, and it's all because you kept us alive

147

and safe."

I went to stand up and Travis grabbed my hand and pulled me back down.

"Whoa there, cowboy. As much as I'm enjoying the fact that you are finally recognizing my awesomeness, I think you might want to take it easy."

"Why? I'm doing great."

"You're scaring me." Travis cocked his head as we heard the faint sound of sirens in the distance. "Here comes the cavalry."

Chapter Twenty-Three

At the hospital the doctors confirmed my belief in Travis's legendary status. Griffin took a little more convincing and had bailed up a doctor in my room.

"Are you sure she's okay?"

I smiled apologetically at the stressed doctor and gripped Griffin's hand, more to give her a free path to the door than for any other reason.

"I'm perfectly fine. Travis did a great job in minimizing the damage to us both."

"I'm going to have to be grateful to him, aren't I?" grumbled Griffin.

"At the very least. You may have to send him a gift basket."

Griffin gave me a small smile and gathered me tightly in his arms. I sighed happily. In that moment before we hit the tree, this was what had been going through my head.

I felt Griffin's arms tighten and heard a throat being cleared at the doorway.

"Can I talk to you, Trudie? Alone."

One thing I had to say about Paul was he didn't lack courage. Trying to tear Griffin away from me after a life threatening incident was not something that a person should do lightly.

I tapped him gently on the arm. "It's okay, this won't take long."

Griffin looked down at me and I waited for his decision.

He kissed me lightly on the forehead. "I'll be right outside. One word from you and I'm back in here."

I knew that. I knew that Griffin would always be there for me. It was one of the many reasons I was marrying him.

Paul stepped back as Griffin walked past him and I could see the way he swallowed nervously. I had to give him credit. Despite no encouragement from me and open hostility from everyone else he had met in this country, he was still determined to put his case forward.

"You really do love him, don't you?"

"Yes, I do." There was no other way to say it. "Why are you here, Paul? I mean, really here? I can't believe that you decided we should get back together all of a sudden."

Paul sat on the edge of the bed. "There is one thing in my life that I am truly ashamed of and that is how I treated you after your accident. I have no defense except that I panicked."

"But why does that translate into insisting that we get back together?"

"Part of it is because I do still love you."

"But that's only a small part, isn't it?"

Paul nodded. "I think part of it is because I'm so ashamed of what I did that I feel like I owe you a husband."

"Paul," I said gently. "That is the most stupid thing I have ever heard you say and I knew you during your teenage years. You do not owe me anything. The fact you were able to walk away should prove that we weren't meant to be together."

Paul looked down at the ground. "Do you hate me for what I did?"

I shook my head. "I don't hate you. After I had some time to think clearly about it I realized that the last thing in the world that I wanted was for you to stay with me because you felt you had to. I wanted to share my life with someone who adored me. Someone who would be by my side through anything because there was nowhere else he would want to be."

"And this new guy is like that?"

I couldn't help the smile that crossed my face. "Yeah."

Paul stood up and ducked his head to kiss me on the cheek. "I think it's time I went home."

"I think that would be a good idea."

Paul gave me a regretful smile as he left the room. Through the open door I saw him go up to Griffin and they spoke quietly.

"What was that about?" I asked Griffin when he returned to my side.

"Just making sure we all knew where we stood."

I groaned. "Please tell me that you didn't threaten him."

"Now that would not be becoming of an officer of the law, would it?"

"That wasn't an answer."

"No, it wasn't." Griffin gave me one of those smiles of his. "You ready to go?"

"Go where?"

"To the station. Pickett has arrested the guy who ran you off the road."

"Already?" I grabbed my bag and stood up quickly.

"Your grandmother called as soon as he started pushing you off the road. We were able to track him through cameras and a police helicopter that was around at that time. Pickett's been interrogating him for the last hour.

"What are you waiting for?"

Standing with Travis and Griffin and watching the suspect in the interrogation room, I couldn't help but feel confused.

"Who is that and what did we do to tick him off so much?"

"His name is Aldo Young."

Travis and I both looked blankly at Griffin.

"About ten years ago he was represented by Martin Harrington."

I could see where this was going.

"Did you by any chance tell anyone that you had

evidence that Harrington was embezzling money?"

"We questioned Martha about whether she knew about Martin embezzling. Dorothy and Eugene were also there. Bernie Deskin gave us the file, but I don't see him calling Martin Harrington and telling him he'd just turned over evidence against him."

A uniformed officer came in the room and nodded at Griffin. "Martin Harrington has just joined us." From the gleeful look on Griffin's face I was pretty sure that his presence was not voluntary. "Hopefully he'll be able to provide some answers for us."

Travis and I waited in the hallway while Griffin started his interrogation of Martin Harrington.

"This got complicated fast, didn't it?"

Travis chuckled. "It always does when you're around. I can see you keeping Griffin on his toes for a very long time."

"I hope so," I said fervently.

As I looked over I saw Avery Harrington was also waiting at the other end of the hallway.

"Wait here a minute," I murmured.

Travis glanced up and I could see he knew exactly what I was doing.

"Not a good idea," he warned.

"Couldn't hurt."

Travis shook his head. "You say that like you really believe it."

I smiled as I went to sit down next to Avery Harrington. If I hadn't been told they were brothers, I would never have guessed. Where Martin was brash and brutish, Avery was slight and quiet.

"I saw you at Dorothy Stanhope's house. I'm her assistant, Trudie Eyre." I stuck my hand out and waited as he hesitantly took it.

"I thought you would be in with your brother."

Avery shook his head. "Martin prefers to use another one of our partners for his own cases."

I stopped myself from wincing. That must be a slap in the face.

"Maybe he doesn't want you to be burdened with the pressure of defending him."

Avery looked at me as if I was crazy. "No, I'm just not a good lawyer and he knows it."

There really was no answer to that.

"It's not like I ever wanted to be a lawyer in the first place." I could feel Avery studying me carefully. "You're the one who found the body."

I nodded, wondering where this conversation was going.

"That's where this whole disaster started."

I couldn't really defend myself, although I was pretty sure that Bernie Deskin had not intended to wait too much longer before exposing Martin Harrington's embezzling.

Avery ran his fingers through his hair. "What a mess."

I had to agree with him there. I looked up to find Detective Pickett motioning for me to go over to him.

"Aldo Young has given a full confession for running you off the road on Martin Harrington's orders."

"Okay."

"We got onto it pretty fast so he didn't have a lot of wiggle room."

I could see Pickett was trying to get me to forgive him for some of his previous actions. I contemplated for a moment to see if we were there yet. Nope. Capturing a guy who had forced me off the road did not make up for using me as bait for a murderer. It was going to take a long time before I got past that. I was surprised. I had always thought of myself as a forgiving person. It seemed I had a limit and Detective Pickett had blasted through it.

I could still give credit where it was due. "That's great. Thanks for finding him so quickly."

Pickett smiled before heading down the hallway.

"He looked happy."

I hadn't heard Travis coming up behind me.

"It seems the driver of the SUV has confessed and he's claiming that Martin Harrington made him do it."

"So, what's Martin Harrington got to say about it?"

"Don't know yet. They're still interrogating him."

The door to the interrogation room opened and every cop in the place turned to watch Martin Harrington being led out in handcuffs. He barely acknowledged his brother. While everyone was watching Martin, I watched as Avery made his way out the building with his head bowed.

Griffin walked over to us with a smile that matched the one on every other cop's face.

"He's been embezzling from the Stanhope estate for years. That paperwork from Bernie Deskin was pretty thorough. He admitted to calling Aldo Young to run you and Cooper off the road and get any evidence you had collected. He thought you were getting too close to the truth."

"Any chance he killed Johnny?"

Griffin sighed. "That would make it very nice and neat, but he's insisting that he didn't."

There was a shock. The criminal was maintaining his innocence.

"So what happens now?"

Griffin looked towards the front of the building. "Now, we question his accomplice."

I followed his line of sight and my jaw dropped as I watched Martha being led into the station with her hands in handcuffs.

"You have got to be kidding me."

Griffin shook his head. "According to Martin, after you spoke to Martha she got onto him and ordered him to have you taken care of. It seems she helped Harrington set up the embezzlement all those years ago. She's been profiting from it quite nicely. You're looking at one very wealthy woman."

"Now I understand why she wasn't upset about losing her job and her home," murmured Travis.

"Are you trying to tell me that Martha Robbins is some criminal mastermind who is able to order someone to kill on her command?"

"That's the premise we're working with."

"Is Martin saying that she killed Johnny Moretti?"

"He won't answer that question. That was the point where he ended the interview."

Pickett came down the hallway. "You ready for this?"

"Sure." Griffin turned to me. "You okay to make your way home?"

"I may need to grab a cab. Travis's car is toast and I left mine at the funeral home this morning."

Griffin pulled some keys out of his pocket which I could have sworn had been in my bag. "I got an officer to drive it over. It's sitting out the back."

I grabbed the keys and gave him a quick peck on the cheek. "You're wonderful. Have fun breaking the evil crime queen."

Griffin waved as he walked off. "Sure I will. Stay out of trouble."

Travis whistled through his teeth. "Why do I get the feeling that he says that to you a lot?"

Chapter Twenty-Four

Waking up the next morning, I smiled over at Griffin who was already getting dressed.

"How late did you get in last night?"

"About midnight. You were fast asleep so I didn't want to wake you up."

"How did Martha's interrogation go?"

Griffin stopped buttoning his shirt. "That woman is cold. There was no way we were going to break her. She's going to fight this thing to the bitter end."

"Did she kill Johnny?"

"She's not admitting to it. According to her, she was supposed to meet him after he dumped Dorothy. He never showed."

"She didn't wonder or care what had happened to him?"

Griffin shook his head. "Like I said, cold."

"So, we're still no closer to finding out who killed Johnny Moretti."

Griffin sat on the bed and put an arm around me. "This is the problem with a case this old. Unless we get a confession we are never going to know who killed him."

"That sucks."

"I know but sometimes life isn't fair. If it makes you feel any better we are going to nail Martha and Martin on the embezzlement charges and conspiracy to murder."

"It only makes me feel a little bit better."

"Better than nothing." Griffin lifted himself off the bed. "What are you doing today?"

"Back to Dorothy Stanhope's house. I still have a job to do."

Griffin stopped walking towards the door. "Just be careful, please.

"I'm always careful." I chose not to be offended by the expression on his face.

After Griffin left, I wandered out to the kitchen to find Grandma Rita making pancakes. I eagerly grabbed a stack.

"I have missed these so much," I sighed blissfully as I demolished the first of many.

Grandma Rita smiled. "You always did appreciate when someone cooked for you." She watched me carefully. "Paul left this morning."

I stopped chewing. "Good. I think he just needed to know it was finished and I didn't hold any bad feelings toward him."

"Your new man seems pretty devoted to you. I was worried. Your mother wasn't overly impressed with him."

I put the fork on the plate. "My mother needs to give Griffin a break. He hasn't done anything to warrant the way she is with him."

"Except take you away."

"What are you talking about?"

Grandma Rita smiled. "I think your mother knew the second she met him that Jake Griffin would be the one man who wouldn't give you up. The fact that he lives on the other side of the world means you won't be coming home except for occasional holidays. For a mother, that's enough to dislike a man. Of course, she also thinks he's the one who gets you in trouble all the time.

"Do you believe that?"

Grandma Rita smiled. "Lord no, girl. If this trip has proved anything it is that you are perfectly capable of getting into trouble all on your own."

"And that's the message I want you to take home to Mom."

Grandma Rita laughed but then quickly sobered. "I'm going home tomorrow."

I paused with a fork in the air. "What are you talking about? You just got here. I haven't had any time with you."

"I only came to help you with the Paul situation and that seems to be taken care of. I'm getting messages that your grandfather's lost without me."

"He's always lost without you but he survives. He'll cope if you take another week or so."

Grandma Rita put her hand on mine. "I miss him. Lord knows that man drives me crazy at times, but not having him next to me just doesn't feel right. One day we'll both come and we can spend more time then."

I squeezed her hand. I understood.

"I have to go into work today, but I'll try to leave early so I can spend the afternoon with you."

"That would be lovely."

When I got to Dorothy Stanhope's house I was surprised to see Travis had beaten me into work and was talking to Dorothy and Eugene.

"What's going on?" I asked Travis.

"We're just discussing what Dorothy's legal options are regarding the embezzlement."

"Okay, I'll be up in the attic if you need me."

It felt good to return to doing the job that I had been hired to do. For just a short amount of time I was able to forget how unhappy this house had been for so long. With the exposure of the secrets and lies, maybe Dorothy had a chance to find some peace.

"How are you doing?" I hadn't expected too much time would pass before Travis interrupted me.

"Fine, how are things going down there."

Travis shrugged as he sat across from me on the floor.

"Dorothy's a bit shocked by everything that has happened, but I can see some strength there. I think she's depending on Eugene a lot right now and he's relishing the job of protector."

I really hoped that Dorothy would be able to trust Eugene. A look must have crossed over my face.

"In answer to the question we've all had since discovering that Martha made her way through pretty much all the men in this household sixty years ago, Eugene claims he never slept with her."

"Do you believe him?" I couldn't hide the skepticism in my voice.

"Actually, I do. I've asked a lot of men that question and had a lot of them lie to me. Usually my instincts are pretty good and my instincts tell me that he never went there."

I breathed out a sigh of relief. I don't know if any of us could have handled the blow if we found out Eugene was another of Martha's conquests.

"So, what do we have with our original case?"

"We know that Martin Harrington got one of his clients to run us off the road, and we have a healthy suspicion that he had something to do with Johnny Moretti's death."

"That isn't enough, is it?" I asked quietly.

"Not even close."

Travis looked defeated. I didn't like that. It just didn't suit him very well.

"But he's still going to jail for trying to get us killed." I tried to make that sound like a positive. From the glum look on Travis's face, I didn't think it worked very well.

"That isn't enough," said Travis.

"What do you mean?"

Travis sighed a little impatiently. "What I mean is that conspiracy to commit murder will get me a hearty slap on the back. If I can pin a murder on Martin Harrington I will never have to pay for a drink in any cop bar in this city ever again."

Once more I found that I was disturbed at discovering where Travis's priorities seemed to lay.

"And Martha?" I queried.

"That woman is damaged beyond repair. Imagine spending your whole life with the sole focus being revenge for something that happened when you were a child. With the embezzlement she had accumulated enough money to leave here years ago. She enjoyed watching Dorothy's life fall apart." Travis shook his head in disgust. "They're going for the same charges as Harrington, but there is nothing to implicate her in Moretti's murder."

I rubbed my hand over my face. "What you're saying is we have two brilliant suspects for Johnny Moretti's murder, but there is no way we can prove it was either of them."

"That about covers it."

"This is so frustrating."

"Welcome to police work."

It was no wonder Griffin got so annoyed sometimes.

We were interrupted by my phone ringing.

"If it's Griffin, tell him that we need some fresh ideas," Travis called out as he lay on his back looking up at the ceiling.

I was smiling when I answered the phone but it wasn't Griffin. After a very short conversation I put my phone back in my bag and nudged Travis with my foot. "Avery Harrington wants to speak to us."

"I wasn't expecting that. Did he say what he wanted to talk to us about?"

"No, just that he wanted to speak to us. I told him we'd meet at his office."

Travis hesitated. "Maybe we should think about this. His brother did try to have us killed yesterday."

He did have a point. "So, what are you saying?"

"I'm just saying that we should be careful."

"Careful as in not going or careful as in taking an armed escort."

Travis looked at me quizzically. "You really are a person of extremes."

"No, I'm a person who is not used to dealing with family members of people who try to kill me. You're supposed to be the expert in these matters."

Travis shrugged. "I'm armed, the Harrington office is a pretty busy place. As long as you run if I tell you to, we should be fine."

I could live with that.

At the office I went to get out of the car and Travis put a hand on my arm to stop me.

"By the way, don't eat or drink anything that he offers to you."

I am sure the expression on my face was horrified.

"You think he'd poison us."

Travis shrugged. "I'm just being cautious."

I could not tell if he was serious or not.

Chapter Twenty-Five

After being ushered into Avery Harrington's office, I was shocked by how drawn he looked. He hadn't looked great the day before, but today he looked like he was collapsing under a heavy load. The only movements were his fingers tapping on the desk. I took a seat across from him and Travis remained standing. For a short time there was silence in the room except for that tapping.

I cleared my throat. "You asked us to come here."

More tapping. I could tell Travis was very close to doing something about that incessant noise. I wasn't inclined to stop him.

"Martin has never liked me."

That wasn't what I thought he'd say but at least the tapping had stopped.

"He was so much older than me and I was desperate for his approval. I followed him everywhere. He used to hit me whenever I got in the way, which was often."

Like I needed another reason to dislike Martin Harrington. I still couldn't see where this was going.

"I never wanted to be a lawyer." He glanced over at me. "I wanted to be a film director."

I looked over at Travis. This was very strange and I wasn't sure why we were here.

"I was always going to become a lawyer because I was a Harrington and that's what we did. I wanted to work in movies."

He smiled at a memory. "When I was ten years old Dorothy Stanhope gave me a movie camera of hers. One of those small ones for home movies." For the first time Avery smiled. "I know she did it because I was Martin's little brother and she was being nice, but that camera meant the world to me."

My heart was beginning to ache for the little boy who'd had a dream and then lost it.

"I made so many home movies. I taped absolutely everything I could." He looked intensely at me. "I think I taped Johnny Moretti's death."

I glanced over at Travis who had stepped closer. "What do you mean you think you taped Johnny Moretti's murder?" he asked.

Avery pulled a small film reel out of his drawer.

"I was hiding from Martin at Dorothy's house when I heard an argument. I started taping but I couldn't really see what was happening. I never saw Johnny after that."

You never looked at what was on the tape?" I couldn't hide the disbelieving note in my voice.

"I was ten years old and what happened that day scared me. My father took the camera away from me not long after that because he didn't want me getting distracted. I kept all the films hidden." He looked at the reel wistfully. "I don't know why. Maybe it was to remind me that I used to dream a long time ago."

I pointed towards the film. "You do realize that this may implicate your brother."

Avery nodded. "I wouldn't be surprised."

"Then why are you doing it?"

"I don't know. I thought I had put that whole situation out of my mind years ago. When I found out Johnny Moretti's body had been found, I stopped being able to sleep."

Avery looked up at us and the only word for the expression on his face was haunted.

"I need to be able to sleep again."

I closed my hand around the film and put it in my bag. "Thank you. We will make sure it goes to the right people."

Travis and I walked out of the office silently. It wasn't until we sat in the car that we turned to each other.

"Do you really think this could have the murder on it?"

Travis shrugged. "He was pretty young when it happened. It could be anything."

"We need to watch it."

"Do you know where we can get hold of a projector for that thing? We're talking technology that's over sixty years old."

"I know exactly where we can find one. I saw one in the attic at Dorothy's house."

"You'd better call Griffin," Travis said as he pulled smoothly into traffic. "If we're about to watch a murder play out on-screen, I really don't want to do it twice."

By the time Griffin and Pickett arrived at the mansion, Travis and I had located the old projector and lugged it downstairs. We had been fortunate that Eugene had some experience with it because Travis and I had put it on the table and didn't have a clue how to set it up.

While Travis and Eugene tinkered I sat down next to Dorothy. "You don't have to be here."

Dorothy gave me a watery smile. "If it gives me the answers to finally put this whole thing to rest, I do need to be here." She looked over at the film reel as it lay on the table. "I remember giving that camera to Avery. He was so little but he loved movies. It was an older camera and someone had given me a brand new one to replace it. I remember him looking at it with such wonder. I didn't think about it once after that day. What if that poor child did tape Johnny's death? That's terrible."

I couldn't argue with her.

Griffin came over and pulled me aside. "Would you listen if I asked you not to watch this?"

"What are you talking about? I want to know who killed Johnny."

Griffin rubbed his hand over his face. "Honey, there is a big difference between knowing who killed someone and seeing it happen. You can't unsee something like that."

"I understand." I did understand. Griffin was doing what he always did, trying to protect me. Just like I had been doing with Dorothy.

"We're ready to go," Eugene announced.

"I'm staying."

Griffin nodded sharply. "If it gets too much, just walk out."

As the flickering images came on the screen it was like we were transported back to a completely different world. It was obvious that the filming had been done by a child. At times it was difficult to tell what was happening.

I heard Dorothy gasp and on the film you could see Martin Harrington with his arms around a woman. The angle was strange so it seemed logical to assume that Avery had been hiding when he was filming this.

"That's my mother."

I glanced over at Travis. I had to give the man credit for his instincts. Even through the degraded quality of the film you could see they were having an affair.

The tryst was interrupted when a smaller young man happened upon them.

"That's Johnny," Dorothy murmured.

There was no sound but it was clear that an argument had broken out. Martin and Johnny started shoving each other. Martin was clearly bigger and stronger, but Johnny was not giving up. He landed what could only be described as a lucky punch. Martin Harrington ended up flat on his back with Johnny standing over him.

An audible gasp went through the room when Dorothy's mother picked up a large object and swung it at Johnny's head. We couldn't hear the point of contact but it still made us wince. Johnny Moretti sank to the floor.

I looked over at Dorothy and saw tears streaming down her face. Eugene had his arm around her and was murmuring in her ear.

On the screen Martin Harrington scrambled up. After a short and obviously intense conversation he picked up the limp form of Johnny Moretti and threw him over his shoulder. The two of them walked out of frame. For several long minutes the camera focused on that one spot until the film ran out.

Griffin broke the silence. "Do we know what that was that she hit him with?

"It's a statue. I recognize it from the attic. I'll go get it now." I felt a bit shaky as I pushed myself out of my chair.

"I'll go with you." Pickett quietly followed me to the attic.

"I never thought this one was going to be solved," he murmured as I made my way to the pile of items that I had already sorted.

"The murderer's already dead. Does it make any difference if they can't be punished?" I knew I was being a bit harsh.

"Johnny Moretti's family and friends are going to know what happened to him. It should give them some peace. In the end that's really all that matters."

Pickett was right.

"There it is." I pointed towards a statue. When I had found the stone carving of an elephant I had thought it was a bit strange. Amongst all of the movie memorabilia it had stood out as an oddity. Now I knew why it had been left in the attic.

Picket pulled on a pair of gloves. "I'll get it."

"That thing is going to have my fingerprints all over it."

"At this stage I think we just want to see if we can confirm it being the murder weapon."

"Lucky I didn't clean it yet."

Pickett grinned.

When we returned to the others I found that Dorothy and Eugene were no longer in the room.

"She wants us all to leave," Travis said in reply to my query. "Don't blame her really. In the short amount of time we've been here her whole world has come tumbling down."

I wondered if that was going to prove to be a good thing or a bad thing.

After Griffin and Pickett left with the evidence I turned to Travis. "I just want to check that she's okay before I leave."

"I didn't expect anything different."

We found Dorothy and Eugene sitting in the garden among the roses that Eugene had tended so diligently and that Dorothy now seemed to enjoy so much.

"Is there anything you need me to do?"

Dorothy smiled tightly. "I think I need some time to work out what I want to do with all this." She looked over at Eugene. "I always wanted to travel."

"I think that would be a great idea."

Dorothy stood up and hugged me. "Thank you for everything you've done."

I wasn't sure if I deserved that.

"I hope she's going to be okay," I said to Travis as we stood next to my car.

Travis shrugged. "Who knows? At least she knows the truth now and she isn't living in some fantasy."

I got into my car. "You did really well on this case. I have to admit, I was very impressed."

Travis grinned. "Remember that for next time."

"There's not going to be a next time."

"Sure, you keep believing that."

Chapter Twenty-Six

I wasn't at home long when Griffin walked through the door.

"Where is everybody?"

"Miss Betsy took Grandma out for the morning to see the 'real Hollywood'.

Griffin grimaced. "Please don't make me be the one to bail them out of whatever they get into."

My smile stopped when I saw the expression on his face. "What's wrong?"

Griffin pulled me down to the couch. "Martin Harrington told us everything that happened."

I waited quietly.

"According to him, Virginia Stanhope hated Johnny Moretti. She thought he was going to convince Dorothy to give up her life as a movie star."

"It was premeditated?"

"That's the thing. She'd talked in broad terms about getting rid of him, but had never actually come up with a plan. At least not one she shared with Harrington."

"She took advantage of a situation."

"Looks like it. Harrington was denying the whole thing even happened until we showed him the film. Then he jumped onto the fact he didn't kill Johnny."

"He's saying he's innocent?"

"Definitely not. We'll be charging him with accessory. A cursory examination of the statue found some very old blood stains and hair. We're sure that it's the murder weapon. We might be able to push for manslaughter. It just depends how brave the prosecutor is feeling, or how much he wants to hurt Martin Harrington. That man has made some enemies."

"Has Rosa Moretti been told?"

Griffin nodded. "Pickett was going to speak to her."

"At least she'll know what happened."

Griffin put his arms around me and pulled me close.

"Are you okay?" he asked quietly into my hair.

"No," I said, "I'm not okay. This wasn't fair. How could her mother do that to her?"

Griffin shrugged. "Maybe she thought she was acting out of a mother's love."

I shook my head. "That wasn't love. That was selfishness. Just because she didn't like him, and didn't think he was good enough for her daughter, does not give her the right to do something so horrible. God knows my mother isn't fond of you, but she's not going to destroy my happiness because of it."

Griffin looked pained. Maybe I shouldn't have brought up my mother's ability to hold a grudge.

"Your grandmother likes me though, that has to count for something."

I laughed and pulled away from him, relieved to break the tension. "My grandmother would love you purely to irritate my mother. You were always going to win there."

I walked into the kitchen and started making a coffee.

Griffin followed me. "Is your job finished at the Stanhope house yet?"

I shrugged. "I'm not sure yet. With everything that happened with the embezzlement they may need to do an audit to see where she can pull some money from. I'm guessing there are going to be court cases to get through. I'll have to talk to Monique to find out what the new plan is."

"Are you still going to take some time off to organize the wedding?"

He said it calmly but I could tell there was some anxiety behind that question.

I froze and I could feel Griffin's eyes on me. I had said that I would take some time to organize this wedding, but I suddenly realized that wasn't what I wanted to do.

I leaned over the bench and grasped his hands between mine. "I want to marry you." I looked into his eyes and hoped that he could feel what I was saying.

Griffin smiled. "I think I already asked you that."

I shook my head. "No, I want to marry you now. I don't want the big wedding, I just want you."

Griffin came around the bench and stood in front of me.

"Are you serious?" he said.

I nodded my head mutely. Everything in me finally felt right. I refused to let my past rule me any more. I loved this man and I wanted to spend the rest of my life with him. Probably driving him completely out of his mind for the rest of his, but for today I was going to focus on the positive side of things.

Griffin grabbed our phones and passed mine over.

"Call everyone you want to be there. I've got a favor owed to me by the County Clerk's office. I'm calling it in."

By the time Grandma Rita and Miss Betsy arrived back at the apartment, wedding plans were in full swing. Despite his reluctance to associate with anything matrimonial, Tomas had jumped in and dragged Helena with him. Most normal people would hesitate at having a funeral cosmetician do the make-up and hair for their wedding. I embraced it. My boss, Monique, arrived at the apartment with a knee-length dress that fit perfectly, just as I expected her to. Two hours later I was more than ready to go.

Standing with Griffin in front of our friends and family in the small room allocated to weddings at the County Clerk's office, I knew I had made the right decision. As we gripped each other's hands tightly I smiled up into the face of the man who I loved with my whole being. His voice was strong and sure as he recited his vows. When he was told to kiss his bride, joy lit up his eyes. His kiss swept me away and I could not stop the wide smile on my face. As soon as the kiss ended, Grandma Rita swept me into her arms.

"I'm so happy for you, sweetheart." She grinned wickedly. "Your mother is going to hate that I was here and she wasn't."

Trust my grandmother to focus on the one downside to being spontaneous.

When Griffin smiled at me I realized it didn't matter. I knew my mother. After she ranted for a bit, she would understand. Sometimes you needed to reach out and grasp happiness with both hands.

About The Author

Leonie Gant started her writing career at the age of ten when she stuffed notes in her pencil case full of ideas for mysteries that Nancy Drew and the Hardy Boys should really have been solving. After years of watching mysteries play out in her head, she decided that writing them down was the best way to deal with them.

In her life away from writing, she is a voracious reader with not nearly enough time to make her way through all the books that she wants to read. She enjoys bushwalking, sewing and chocolate, possibly not in that order. She also believes in the value of trying new things, walking in the rain and enjoying every moment.

To find out more about Leonie Gant and her books
www.leoniegant.com

Discover other titles by Leonie Gant
Not Famous in Hollywood
Not Happily Married in Hollywood
Not Talented in Hollywood
Not Wanted in Hollywood
Not Suspicious in Hollywood